ie **Metcalfe** lives in Cornwall with her
-suffering husband, four children and
horses. When she was an army brat,
ently on the move, books became the
friends that came with her wherever
ent. Now that she writes them herself
making new friends, and hates saying
e at the end of a book—but there are
more characters in her head,
ing for attention until she can't wait
eir stories.

tles by the same author:

GED-FOR BABY*
XPECTED CHILD*
TOR, LIKE SON

Doctors

Dear Reader

As a member of a large f
imagine how single mum J
have felt when she lost h
and believed that she
Natasha were all alone
discovered her moth
secret.

Armed with the na
fathered her, she w
she'd never known
half-siblings, Da
before she co
approach them
going to be w
man who ha
first time sh
medical sc'
that filled
they wor'
thrown
her pre
out of

She
dau
ne
h

Jos
long
two
frequ
only
she w
she is
goodb
always
clamou
to tell th

Recent ti

HIS LON
HIS UNEX
LIKE DOC
*The ffrench

HER
LONGED-FOR
FAMILY

BY
JOSIE METCALFE

MILLS & BOON®

First published in Great Britain 2006
Large Print edition 2006
Harlequin Mills & Boon Limited,
Eton House, 18-24 Paradise Road,
Richmond, Surrey TW9 1SR

© Josie Metcalfe 2006

ISBN-13: 978 0 263 18894 3
ISBN-10:   0 263 18894 9

Set in Times Roman 16¼ on 21 pt.
17-1106-51637

Printed and bound in Great Britain
by Antony Rowe Ltd, Chippenham, Wiltshire

CHAPTER ONE

'HEY, Nick! Love the tan! How far does it go?' Libby's companion said to someone over her shoulder, a teasing grin on her face. 'A and E hasn't been the same without your gorgeous bod around. Welcome back.'

The answering chuckle was deep and resonant and struck an unexpectedly responsive chord inside Libby.

Curious, she turned to find herself looking up a long way past broad shoulders into a face composed entirely of lean planes and angles. As Sally had said, he looked tanned and healthy with the sort of burnished blond hair that she usually associated with keen outdoorsmen rather than respectable doctors. His smile was wide and was complemented by sparkling blue eyes that crinkled enticingly at the corners as he shared the joke.

Then he caught sight of her and literally in the blink of an eye his expression changed, all humour wiped away as though it had never been.

'Libby?' He sounded almost shocked. *'Libby Cornish?'*

Well, he clearly knew her at first glance, she realised, struck by a sudden scary return to those days when she hadn't been able to rely on her memory. It might have been more than eight years ago, but there were still times when she came up against the black hole into which several weeks of her life had disappeared almost without trace.

Conscious that there was now a circle of interested faces waiting to see how this apparent reunion progressed, she gave herself a silent shake and forced herself to focus. There couldn't be many people with that same combination of sun-streaked blond hair and deep blue eyes in a bone structure that hinted at Scandinavian or Slavic ancestry, but why someone this gorgeous would ever remember such a little brown wren as herself...

'Nick?' she questioned, repeating the name Sally Nugent had called him, but somehow it didn't fit with the image that was emerging from the disorganised store of memories. Nicholas was far too ordinary for someone who looked like...

'Kolya!' she exclaimed as several missing pieces of jigsaw suddenly slotted into place. How could she have forgotten the man who had featured in so many of her daydreams during the first half of her medical training? And where had her brain gleaned the information that Kolya, rather than Nick, was his family's diminutive for Nikolai? In spite of her longing, she certainly hadn't been close enough to him eight years ago for any personal conversations, so her greatest surprise was still that he'd remembered her at all.

'It's Howell... Nick Howell, not Collier,' Sally corrected, but Libby didn't bother explaining that she hadn't been guessing at his surname… Neither did the silent man now looking down at her with a distinct lack of welcome on his face.

'We started at medical school together,' Libby babbled into the uncomfortable pause, wondering what on earth had put that cold expression there. It certainly couldn't be anything in her references from her previous job. They'd been excellent. And as for any lingering animosity from their student days…well, it couldn't be anything like that. As far as she could remember, she'd barely done more than worship the man from afar while he'd been all but oblivious of her existence. 'Up to the middle of third year, that is, when I had my…accident and transferred to a med school closer to home.'

Damn. She hadn't intended mentioning that at all. It certainly wasn't relevant to the job she was doing here and she really didn't want to give her new colleagues any reason to doubt her skills. If she hadn't been so rattled by his strange attitude towards her…

'Accident? What accident?' Nick's voice was

sharp and his eyes weren't expressionless now. There was that light in them that had always signalled that his supremely analytical mind was at work. She had noticed that right from the start of his training.

'Nick. Libby. You can catch up with all the gossip during your break,' decreed the senior sister before Libby could answer, and she breathed a silent sigh of relief. She really didn't want the whole department listening in while she rehashed the most ghastly time in her life. She'd rather not talk about it at all.

'The board is filling up and we don't want a department overflowing with minor injuries in case we get a run of emergencies coming in,' Kelly Sissons went on briskly before she shooed the rest of them away. 'Nick, as the two of you already know each other, it saves me making the introductions. Would you and Libby do a stint in minors to see if we can clear it out? It all seems to be much the usual mix of cases. I'll call you if we need more hands at the majors end of the department.'

Nick executed a smiling salute then set off along the corridor, leaving Libby to follow in his wake with the memory of the fact that, once again, his smile had faded when he'd looked in her direction.

'What *is* his problem?' she muttered under her breath, cross that her pleasure in her new job was being spoiled by her former colleague's attitude. She was tracking him with her eyes as he drew steadily ahead of her, his long legs making short work of the distance. That had been another of the ways in which the two of them had been so different eight years ago, and nothing had changed. He'd been the tall, good-looking young man who would have topped any popularity poll, whereas she was short and so nondescript that people could trip over her before they noticed her. At least she didn't still weigh twice what she should. That was one small improvement on her medical student self.

'Oh, good. Reinforcements!' exclaimed a rather harassed-looking nurse when Nick shouldered his way into the minor injuries unit. '*Two* of you? This must be my lucky day.'

'I can't guarantee that you'll have us *that* long,' Nick warned, but she waved off the caution.

'I know you'll be out of here like a shot if something juicier comes up,' she grumbled, then gave the two of them an evil grin. 'That's why I'm going to get my money's worth out of you while you're here. I'm going to keep sending them through as fast as I can until you shout for mercy! They don't call me Connie the Barbarian for nothing!'

Libby chuckled as she followed the beckoning finger, glad that she'd had a couple of days to get to know her way around all the separate areas of the department. She certainly wouldn't want to be fumbling her way around under Nick's glowering expression.

'Libby, your embroidery's good, so you can take the head laceration in three,' Connie directed. 'Nick, there's a dislocation waiting for reduction in two that could give your muscles a workout.'

Without another word he turned and disappeared into his assigned area and Libby drew a relieved breath as she pulled on a pair of disposable gloves and introduced herself to the young man waiting to have his head wound sutured.

She'd relaxed too soon, she realised when the rumble of Nick's deep voice travelled all too easily across the few yards that separated them and wrapped itself around her jangling nerves.

'How did this happen?' she asked her burly patient to distract him as she delivered a series of injections of local anaesthetic into the edges of a jagged head wound. Out of the corner of her eye she caught the young nurse's grimace and wondered whether this was her first stint in Accident and Emergency. This looked as if it was going to be a complicated job to get a good result and the last thing she needed was a nurse who couldn't bear looking at gory injuries.

Well, she'd find out as soon as the local anaesthetic took effect because she'd be asking the pale-faced young woman to give the whole thing a thorough irrigation before she began the essential debridement.

'I fell off some scaffolding and hit my head on a shackle,' the young man said gruffly, his hands tightening into white-knuckled fists at the groaning sound coming from the direction of the cubicle Nick had entered. 'Listen, that's my mate over there. Is he OK?'

'If you'll promise to stay still for me, I'll ask your nurse if she'll go and find out,' Libby bargained, her last words almost drowned out by a barely muted bellow from nearby.

In the sudden silence that followed, she heard a sound that could only be swearing, although the words were completely incomprehensible. Libby had to stifle a chuckle at the fleeting memory that, in moments of stress, Nick had been known to swear, but only ever in a language distinctly Slavic in origin.

'Can *you* go and find out?' her patient begged, twisting himself out of her reach to look pleadingly up at her. 'If Jason hadn't grabbed me— he caught me one-handed and held on even when his shoulder dislocated—I'd have come off a lot worse than a cut on my head. From five lifts up, I'd probably be dead.'

'You'll have to promise to sit perfectly still when I come back,' Libby bargained sternly as she pushed her wheeled stool back and stood up.

'You help my mate and I'll do whatever you want,' he said seriously as another yell made them all wince.

'Need a hand in here?' she asked as she followed her ears to the nearby cubicle and found a scowling Nick muttering under his breath. 'That was the Russian version of "Excuse my French", I think,' she said in an aside to the grim-faced man lying on the couch. She smiled at Wei Lin, the only nurse in A and E who was even smaller than she was. At the moment, she looked completely out of her depth.

'Well, I wish I could speak it, too,' the patient said through gritted teeth. 'It sounds more impressive than "bloody hell", any day of the week.'

'Won't it go back?' she asked Nick, quite surprised that he hadn't already managed to manoeuvre the joint back into its socket.

'Haven't got that far yet,' he said shortly, positioning the Entonox mask more firmly over the man's face and persuading him to take another series of deep breaths. 'It's taken this long to get enough sedation into him to get him lying down, and Wei Lin is even smaller than you are. With his degree of muscular development it's going to take more than a polite tug to get it to go back.'

'Sorry about the noise,' Jason apologised with a groan hardly muffled even by the oxygen mask. 'I've never had anything hurt so much as this. Couldn't even lie back without this…' he grimaced as he gestured towards his deformed-looking shoulder '…hurting like hell.'

'Wouldn't it be better to reduce it in Theatre?' Libby suggested when she realised that it was probably the sheer bulk of the muscles that the man needed for his work—and which had also given him the strength to save his colleague's life—that were making the problem worse. Nick

was having to pull against those muscles to position the bone to allow it to slip back into joint.

'It would definitely be easier on Jason,' Nick
agreed, 'but there isn't anywhere free for at
least half an hour and we don't have that long.'

'The sooner the better, as far as I'm concerned,' groaned Jason, completely missing
Nick's gesture towards Wei Lin, who was obviously monitoring the pulse in the dislocated
arm. 'But I didn't realise the hospital told you
how long things like this were supposed to take.
Do they time you with stop-watches?'

Not wanting to scare him with the fact that
Nick had picked up that the dislocation was interfering with the supply of blood and possibly
the nerves to the arm, Libby knew that Nick's
concern was that any delay could affect Jason's
ability to use the arm for the rest of his life, but
she sidetracked his attention by joking about his
view that the medical staff were treated little better than employees on a factory production line.

And all the while she was following Nick's
muttered instructions about positioning herself

to assist Wei Lin to counter the pull-and-rotate manoeuvre he was about to perform on the arm.

'Hey, Jason, stop trying to chat the pretty doctor up and take another gulp or two of that gas,' he chided with a deceptive smile when they were positioned to his satisfaction. 'You don't want the pain to come back because you tighten up at the wrong moment, do you?'

'No way!' their patient said fervently and drew in a deep breath. 'I can still *look* at her, though, can't I…?' he added with a cheeky grin on the exhalation.

A scowl darkened Nick's face at the open flirting in his tone, much to Libby's surprise. The Nick she remembered from the days of her infatuation had been every bit as much a flirt, and the welcome he'd received in the department this morning had initially reinforced that impression. Could he really have changed so much in the intervening years or was there something about *her* that put him in a bad mood?

'Ready?' he demanded, cutting into her thoughts, his voice somehow sounding more like the warning growl of a junkyard dog than a medical professional requesting assistance.

Libby leant back, applying a steady counter-acting force as Nick pulled against the power of the muscles of Jason's shoulder girdle and rotated the arm until the ball of the joint was finally in the correct position to slide neatly into the socket with an audible click.

'Have you done it yet?' demanded a groggy Jason several seconds later, his words muffled by the Entonox mask still clamped tightly over his face with his free hand, apparently oblivious to the last few minutes of effort.

Libby watched as Nick checked Jason's pulse to be certain that full circulation had been restored then tested his neurological responses, and only breathed a silent sigh of relief when he nodded.

'All done,' he confirmed as he straightened up. 'Wei Lin will tape your shoulder up to give it some support and stop you using it…'

'Stop me using it!' he exclaimed, clearly horrified. 'But I have to be able to use it to do my job. I can't rig scaffolding one-handed.'

'You won't be rigging scaffolding at all… *ever*…if you don't give that shoulder time to repair,' Nick said flatly. 'The whole joint is badly bruised and there could even be some tearing of muscles and tendons. If you use it before it's mended, you'll make the damage worse.'

'You could even end up needing major surgery to rebuild your shoulder,' Libby added, deliberately describing a worst-case scenario and totally unsurprised when the big man grimaced at the very idea.

'Well, how many days will it take to repair?' he demanded, backing down reluctantly. 'We're up to our necks in work at the moment and there aren't enough qualified riggers in the area as it is.'

'Well, there'll be one less, *permanently*, if you don't take care of that shoulder,' Nick was saying sternly as Libby left him to it, knowing she had her own patient waiting for attention. At least the anaesthetic injections would have had time to take effect, and she'd be able to give him some good news about his rescuer as she stitched his wound.

Except she couldn't keep her mind on what she was doing for more than a moment at a time. Oh, she managed to do a good job of lining up the neatened edges of the gash and she even managed to stitch them together so that the scar would be as unobtrusive as possible. But as for keeping her thoughts under control...that was something out of her power for the first time in a very long time.

And whose fault was that?

Well, it couldn't be Nick's. He'd barely done more than glance in her direction, so he certainly hadn't invited her to notice that the sun that had darkened his skin to such a glowing tan had also given the hairs on his arms the sheen of burnished gold. And as for the breadth of his shoulders and the lean power in the muscles that had tightened into knotted ropes as he had fought to reduce his patient's dislocated arm...

'Right, Jacqui,' she said to the nervous nurse, who had proved far tougher than she'd looked, angry that she was obsessing over the man like this. Had she learned nothing since she'd met him as a teenager? 'Could you put a dressing on that for me and make sure to give him the leaflet about the warning signs for concussion? He'll need an appointment to have the stitches taken out, but that could be done at his GP's surgery if that's more convenient.' She knew she was babbling and had a feeling that Jacqui didn't need any reminders to do that part of her job, but her thoughts were in a tangled mess and that wasn't good enough.

'*Not for this job, it isn't,*' she whispered fiercely as she added her signature to the bottom of the case notes and made her way towards the crowded whiteboard for her next assignment. She knew only too well that even a momentary lack of attention could mean the difference between spotting a life-threatening symptom and missing it entirely.

'Libby.' Nick's determined voice right behind her was enough to scatter her logical thoughts to the wind. 'If you're between patients, I need a word with you.'

Silently, she followed him into the cluttered

office, hoping she looked more composed than she felt. Had she done something wrong? She honestly didn't think she'd been so distracted that she'd missed something important, but...

'What accident did you have that made you change medical schools?' he demanded as soon as the door closed, and momentarily robbed her of the power to breathe.

That was the *last* thing she'd expected him to ask. She'd actually thought he'd forgotten all about it when he hadn't followed up on it. She should have known better. He had a mind like a steel trap when it came to details. 'I was knocked down and spent a couple of days in ICU,' she said simply, deliberately leaving out any details.

'Knocked down! When? Where?' he demanded.

Libby was startled to realise that he wasn't going to be satisfied by the abbreviated version. After all, he'd barely noticed her in those days as she'd kept herself to her studious corner. Well, she could certainly answer his questions but there were some things about that night that she *wasn't* willing to share with him.

'Apparently, I was crossing the road at night, and as I didn't have any identification on me, the hospital I was taken to—not ours, by the way, so that's probably why no one knew where I was—couldn't even tell my mother what had happened. Then, by the time I was fit to return to med school I'd missed too much to continue that year and the dean suggested starting the year again. Anyway, why do you want to know? It happened nearly ten years ago and it's never affected my ability to do my job.'

So many expressions crossed his face that it was difficult to know just what he was thinking. There was shock, obviously. No one liked hearing that a fellow student had been injured. There was also concern, and after all the scowls he'd thrown in her direction since they'd started working together, that unexpected warmth was like balm on her soul.

For just a moment, she actually thought about telling him the whole story, but just couldn't bring herself to do it. This was Nick Howell, the fellow student she'd fantasised about from the moment she'd met him and who was now her superior in the department. She didn't know him well enough to tell him about the long-term results of that night. There was no one she trusted well enough for that.

'There was more to it than you're telling me,' Nick said suddenly, his eyes narrowing, and Libby silently cursed her expressive face. 'But for the moment, I'll take your word for it that it doesn't affect your abilities as a doctor.'

But the strangest thing of all, she realised when she lay in bed later that night, was not that she was remembering Nick as he'd been as an intense but fun-loving medical student or as the endlessly competent sun-kissed A and E doctor she'd encountered today, but that she had a perfectly detailed picture in her mind of exactly the way Nick would look without a stitch of clothing; the way the broad swathe of tawny hair across his chest narrowed as it swooped down towards…

'Pervert!' she whispered to herself when she realised just where her thoughts were going.

'I know what that means,' said a little voice from the bed on the other side of the bedroom, and Libby's eyes widened.

'Tash! Why aren't you asleep?' She sat up instantly, motherly concern overriding everything else. Her daughter was usually fast asleep by now and woke before the alarm went off in the morning.

'I had a pain in my leg that wouldn't let me go to sleep and I heard you talking to yourself. You said the same word my teacher did.'

Pervert? Why on earth had Tash's teacher been talking about perverts to a class of eight-year-olds? She'd had no leaflet home to inform her that the class was having a 'stranger danger' talk.

'We were doing running today and I'm usually the fastest but today my leg just didn't want to run,' her precious child continued. 'Mrs Peverill said I was just being perverse, but I wasn't. My leg was aching and it felt too heavy to go fast.'

Libby's antennae started to twitch as she totted up symptoms, then she realised what she was doing and forced herself to switch out of doctor mode. This was her daughter talking, not one of the patients at the hospital. It was probably nothing more than the result of a knock during some typical eight-year-old rough-and-tumble in the playground.

'Do you want me to kiss it better so you can go to sleep?' Libby offered, knowing that the days when she could make that offer were swiftly drawing to an end. Her little girl was growing up so fast, all long coltish legs and slender body now that she'd put on a growth spurt and lost the last of her baby chubbiness.

It wouldn't be very long before she would want a bedroom of her own and that would mean finding a bigger flat than this tiny box. She winced at the thought of the expense and wondered how her mother had ever managed. At least the new job at St Luke's would give her a steady income, even if it wouldn't stretch as far as she would like to provide everything she wanted for her daughter.

'Will you give me a hug till I go to sleep?' said the little voice in the darkness, and as

Libby hurried to comply, she knew that the need for a second bedroom was a little way off yet, if her precious Tash could still ask for a hug the way she had as a toddler.

'Only if you move that enormous dinosaur out of the way to make room for me,' she teased as she slid under the covers and wrapped her arms round the precious little body. 'There isn't room for all three of us in here.'

Nick collapsed in a boneless heap in his comfortable recliner, glad that the interminable day was finally over, but that didn't mean that he could switch his brain off.

It had been the same all day...ever since he'd looked up from the latest round of Sally's teasing and found himself looking into Libby Cornish's blue-green eyes...her *unforgettable* blue-green eyes, dammit!

It had been more than eight years since the last time he'd seen them, and in spite of the fact that he'd believed himself long since immune to her, she could still make his heart skip a beat.

'Not again!' he growled, wincing at the memories. There was no way he was going to let a slender wraith with sunshine in her hair and the enticing sparkle of laughter in her blue-green eyes wrap herself around his heart only to rip it out by the roots like an unwanted weed. '*Never* again!' he vowed. He'd learned his lesson the first time around and he wasn't a man to repeat his mistakes if he could help it. It wasn't worth the pain.

It was almost a relief to have to drag himself out of his angry introspection to answer the phone.

'Yes!' he snapped, still partially trapped in his angry thoughts, then grimaced guiltily when he heard the familiar voice on the other end.

'*Dobry vecher* to you, too, darling!' said his mother with a little chuckle. 'Bad day, or daren't I ask?'

'The day just got better, Mama,' he said, avoiding a direct answer. 'How are you and Papa? All packed and ready to go?'

'I'm still not certain that we're doing the right thing,' she admitted in her softly accented voice. 'It's so far away and what happens if—?'

'Mama, nothing's going to happen except the two of you are finally taking that trip you've always talked about,' he soothed. 'After all these years, you're finally going to get a chance to practise your rusty Russian on real Russians and catch up on all the family news in person.'

'But your father—'

'Papa will be fine. His doctor has checked him over and he's taking all his medication with him… And, anyway, it's not as if you're going to an uncivilised country. They *do* have hospitals in Russia, don't they?' he teased, knowing what the reaction would be.

'Of *course* they do,' she agreed quickly, predictably stung by even the suspicion of a slur on her native country. 'Very *good* hospitals,' she elaborated, her trace of an accent growing stronger with every word. 'Best in the world…apart from the hospital where you work, Kolya, of course.'

'Of course!' He laughed. 'So, there'll be no more worrying about whether you're doing the right thing. You'll both be fine. I'll be there to pick you up tomorrow morning in plenty of time to take you to the airport.'

'Are you sure you can do that? What about your work? You just took some time off to help us get everything ready to go away…the garden, the new security locks on the windows…'

'That's a change!' he teased. 'Usually, you're telling me not to work too hard. But don't worry. It will only be for a couple of hours and I've got a colleague to cover for me while I see you on your way. I'll pay him back later when he needs some time off.'

'And you? Will you be all right while we're away?'

Nick chuckled. 'I already told you—I'm a big boy, Mama. You don't need to worry about me.'

'Of *course* I worry about you, Kolya. It is a mother's job to worry about her son, especially when he's so alone. You need something in your life apart from your work. Someone who will care for you…a *wife*!' she announced triumphantly. '*That's* what you need. *That's* what I shall do while we're visiting the family. There are so many cousins, second cousins and third cousins that it will be easy to find you a good Russian wife. Then you will be as happy as your papa and not work so hard.'

Nick groaned aloud at the excitement in her voice. 'No, Mama! Don't you dare start matchmaking again. Don't you remember what happened the last time you tried to find me a wife?' He still broke out in a sweat when he remembered the succession of desperate thirty-somethings—everyone from his father's health visitor to his mother's hairdresser—who had seen him as their last chance to hook anything with a y chromosome and a pulse.

'Ah, but this time will be different,' she promised with a happy lilt to her voice. 'They will be *Russian*!'

The only thing Nick was grateful for when the call finally ended was that the idea of finding him a wife had completely banished his mother's fears about the upcoming journey.

The prospect of being bombarded by another batch of man-hungry women was another matter, especially when he had no intention of falling in love. He couldn't blame his mother for wanting him to be happy—any good mother would want that for their child—but why couldn't she accept that he gained all the satisfaction he needed from his work?

Working in A and E was the perfect job for him. He saw the patients just long enough to diagnose their problems and treat them, or to stabilise them sufficiently to send them for further treatment elsewhere. He didn't have time to become attached to them so he was never at risk of having his emotions shredded.

'No, I'm a bachelor by choice,' he declared aloud as he directed his weary feet towards the bathroom, visions of much-needed sleep already beckoning. 'And it doesn't matter how many beautiful Russian relatives Mama sends my way, that's the way I'm going to remain.'

So why was it that as soon as his head hit the pillow, his thoughts returned to the elfin features of the one woman he'd never been able to forget?

'It's just a reminder,' he muttered as he tried unsuccessfully to banish the image. 'It's my brain's way of reminding me that Libby's the perfect example of why I shouldn't get involved.'

CHAPTER TWO

LIBBY took a deep breath before she climbed out of her car the next morning, unexpectedly nervous about seeing Nick again.

'You're just being stupid,' she scolded herself under her breath as she hurried from the car park towards the A and E entrance. 'He's just someone you knew when you were doing your training, and now you're going to be working together. He doesn't know that you lusted after him from the first moment you laid eyes on him, or that your heart still goes crazy at the sight of him...even when he seems to spend his time scowling at you,' she finished as she tried to slide surreptitiously into the back of the room to listen to a swift handover.

'Uh-oh! Watch out, everybody. She's only been

with us a few days and she's already talking to herself,' Sally announced, and Libby was hotly embarrassed to realise that her private pep talk must have been more public than she'd thought.

'I was just...' Libby was totally bereft of words. She had no idea how much Sally had heard and was worried that she might have realised who she'd been talking about. The last thing she needed was to start everyone gossiping, especially when there was nothing to gossip about.

'Sally, don't tease the girl or you'll frighten her away,' Kelly scolded briskly from her position at the front of the room, her dark blue uniform beautifully crisp at the start of the shift. 'Grab those two boxes on the table beside you and pass them around, will you?' Libby turned to discover two bakery boxes laden with sugar-coated doughnuts and saw Sally's eyes light up covetously even as they started distributing the contents.

'Now, if you're all happy boosting your energy levels with a sugar hit, pin back your ears and let's get this over with as quickly as possible.' Kelly paused briefly in the expectation that everyone would be silent, and such was her air of command that, mouths full of the sugary treats or not, all conversation quickly ceased. 'Nick's going to be late in this morning and the night shift had a dreadful time. There's already a backlog of patients waiting for attention in minors, and that's *before* the influx of rush-hour accidents, so we're going to need every pair of hands we've got.'

There was a weary groan from everyone in the room when they realised they were probably going to be playing catch-up for most of the day. That meant a lot of people waiting a long time, often for relatively minor complaints, with the resulting rise in tempers all round.

Kelly swiftly detailed which departments she wanted her troops to cover then did a quick rundown of the patients who were currently undergoing treatment, waiting for blood-test or X-ray results or waiting for consultants to arrive from other departments. To Libby's relief, Sally was going to have to check on the readiness of the resus rooms, but then she heard her name being linked with Nick's again and her relief was short-lived. Once he arrived, it seemed as if she was doomed to spend another long day rubbing elbows with him while they worked to keep the board clear in the minor injuries unit.

'Drat. We're not going to be working together.' Sally threw a teasing grimace at Libby as she hurried to comply. 'When you came in muttering like that I was sure I was on to something juicy. Now I'm not going to have a chance to put you through the third degree to get all the details and there hasn't really been anything to gossip about since Leah Dawson got engaged to David ffrench, and everybody could see that one coming from a mile off.'

'Well, I'm sorry to be so boring,' Libby said with pretended humility as she made her way through the department as quickly as possible without looking as if she was in a hurry to get away from Sally's keen eyes. 'I'm afraid my life revolves around my job and my daughter.'

'Double drat! Definitely nothing to gossip about there—unless your daughter's the secret result of a torrid affair with a world-renowned rock star or something!'

For a second Libby couldn't breathe at the thought that her precious Tash might be tainted by gossip. It took her a second to dredge up an imitation of a carefree laugh. 'Sorry, Sally...no rock stars and no secret affairs,' she said with a shrug, already focusing her eyes on the colour-coded names on the whiteboard at the minor injuries side of the reception area. 'Just the start of another interminable twelve-hour shift patching up bodies.'

Sally groaned. 'Don't remind me! And all without the delectable Dr Howell to brighten our lives. Still,' she continued even as Libby paused, wanting to find a way to ask where the man was without drawing attention to her need to know just how much of a Nick-free day she could look forward to. 'You can hardly blame the man for wanting to see his parents off in person.'

'See them off?' Libby echoed, intrigued. 'Sounds as if he's setting the dogs on them.'

Sally chuckled. 'Nothing so dramatic. Just that he's finally persuaded the two of them to make their trip to Russia.'

Russia? Libby pondered as she cleaned and stitched a jagged tear from a rusty nail sustained by an amateur property developer. Something in the back of her brain told her there was something significant in that destination, but the longer she worried at the thought, the sharper the ache grew inside her head.

She almost groaned aloud with frustration. Why did that always have to happen when she tried to resurrect the memories that had disappeared into the black hole left by her accident?

It didn't matter how often the hospital staff had told her that she shouldn't worry about it. She couldn't help it. They'd told her that the amnesia covered such a short time in her life that it was unlikely she'd forgotten anything of major importance. They'd warned her that it could be her brain's way of protecting her from something she wouldn't want to remember...such as the actual circumstances that had resulted in her running wildly in front of the taxi that had only just avoided killing her.

Not that she could class her lost memory of Nick's connection to Russia in the same category as the event that had resulted in a coma and a stay in ICU that had, at one stage, threatened to be long-term.

But it was frustrating not to know, she brooded as her grateful patient left to pull down the rest of a water-soaked ceiling one-handed before the builder arrived to put up the new one.

Her next patient was the result of a quick call from the major injuries end of the department, a young asthmatic with almost no respiratory sounds at all.

'He was so determined to help his daddy with the bonfire in the garden,' Jake's tearful mother explained as the team worked over the grey-faced child. 'At first, he was all right...when they were burning all the dry stuff and the smoke was going straight up. But then they got to the greener stuff and when the wind picked up and started swirling the smoke around...'

'Then the smoke concentration became more than his inhaler could cope with,' Libby finished for her, anxiously monitoring her small charge for any improvement in his oxygen saturation, no matter how slight. Inside her head she was railing against foolish people who didn't seem to be able to grasp the fact that asthma could be a killer.

'Hey, Jake, how are you doing?' said an all-too-familiar voice behind her, and she silently cursed the way her own pulse rate instantly overtook Jake's on the monitor display. To her surprise, Jake's little hand came up just far enough to meet Nick's in an attempt at a 'high five' even though his eyes didn't open. 'You take it easy, my little friend,' Nick said gently as he stroked his hand over the tousled head. 'You need to get better so you can boss that little sister of yours around. You don't want her to start messing with your toys.'

This time, there was a slight grimace in response to the teasing that corresponded with an improvement of the monitor display. What

Libby didn't know was whether the improvement was purely as a result of the medication and oxygen she'd been giving Jake, or Nick's gentle teasing of a patient who was obviously a regular visitor in the department.

'I'll be back in a minute,' he promised, prompting Jake to open his eyes and try to form a protest. 'Hey, take it easy,' Nick said quickly, giving Jake's hand a squeeze when it seemed as if he was going to get agitated. 'I'm only going to try to track down that computer game. You beat me last time, so you've got to give me a chance to get my own back.'

Libby's eyes were smarting as they met Nick's. When she'd known him before, he'd always been the life and soul of any group, easily the most popular person in their year at medical school. She would never have guessed that he could be so gentle and sensitive where a frightened little boy was concerned.

'Anyway,' he added with a glance in her direction that was totally at odds with the apparently genuine smile that curved his mouth, 'you've got the prettiest doctor in the whole hospital to look after you, so you have to get better quickly.'

Jake threw a wary look in her direction, almost as if he could detect the mismatch between Nick's words and his expression, but the promise of a computer battle won out.

'See you...in a minute,' he wheezed, then settled back against the pillows, one little hand holding the all-important mask in position.

Libby was conscious of the unending queue of people waiting to be seen but was helpless to drag her eyes away from the man.

It had always been like this, right from the first time she'd caught sight of him when the two of them had been registering on their first day at medical school. He'd been laughing with the woman assigned to confirm their details, his teeth very white against skin bronzed by a summer full of sunshine, his blond hair bleached almost to silver where it had fallen towards eyes as blue as the sky and filled with laughter and the sheer joy of living.

Libby's heart had given an excited leap that

had had absolutely nothing to do with the fact that she had finally been embarking on the career she'd always dreamed of and everything to do with her gorgeous fellow student who had looked more like a long, lean, laid-back beach boy than a serious medical student.

He was still long and lean and bronzed, and still moved with that deceptively lazy-looking stride that covered more ground than most men did when they hurried. His shoulders were broader now, but it must be muscle, because he still didn't look as if he had a spare ounce on his whole frame, and as for the way his trousers fitted his...

'Libby? Have you got a minute?' Sally's urgent words broke into her unaccustomed musings and she hastily glanced down at Jake, hoping that neither her little patient nor his mother had noticed her sudden preoccupation with a fellow doctor's more obvious attributes.

'I'm all yours,' she said as she turned to face the waiting nurse. 'What's the problem?'

'Query renal colic,' she said cryptically, drawing Libby just far enough away from the cubicle so that their conversation couldn't easily be overheard, while still leaving her close enough to keep an eye on her fragile little patient and his monitor readings. She certainly couldn't leave him until Nick returned to take over from her. 'He's describing all the classic symptoms—the pain, the location and the fact that he's had episodes before...'

Libby gave her friend a wry smile. 'And he knows exactly what drugs will give him relief, but he's having trouble coming up with the temperature and sweating now that we've got him in here under supervision?'

'Exactly. And he doesn't seem to have been here before. I've checked on the computer records...at least, not under the name he's given us today,' Sally confirmed. 'And without his real name, I can't check to see if he's been treated in any of the other hospitals with records on the system.'

'So, what is St Luke's usual protocol for dealing with someone who could be faking it to score a free dose of Class A drugs?' They both knew that pretending to have renal colic was quite a common ploy used by addicts to try to pull the wool over a busy A and E doctor's eyes.

'Well, I've got him on an Entonox mask, but he wasn't happy when I told him I had to get a doctor to look at him to OK anything stronger.'

'And if he *had* been receiving treatment for renal colic in the past, he would already be in the system. He'd also know that you would have to get one of us to prescribe the necessary drugs, but was probably hoping we would be too busy to do anything more than rubber stamp the drugs request,' Libby finished for her, correctly reading her sceptical expression. 'Did you get the chance to check his arms for needle tracks?' That was the most obvious place to look, but some addicts were all too adept at hiding the injection sites between toes and anywhere else that they thought might escape detection.

'He's got more layers on than an onion, and even though he hasn't taken a single layer off, he still hasn't been able to produce a sweat in spite of the level of heating in the department,' Kelly quipped. 'Best of luck if you're going to try to get him to take enough of those off to get a look at any skin.'

'Well, he'll have two choices,' Libby warned in a voice that only carried as far as the senior sister's ears. She paused just long enough to give Nick an update on Jake's slowly improving readings as he arrived with the elusive computer game, then was able to give Sally her full attention. 'He'll have to strip off for a proper examination or he gets nothing at all.'

'You can't do that, can you?' Sally asked with a worried frown, clearly concerned about the legality of the suggestion. 'It's all about "informed patient consent" these days, isn't it?'

'If *you* don't know the letter of the law, I hope *he* doesn't,' she said softly, and raised crossed fingers. 'In fact, I think I'm going to go for shock tactics to save any more wasted time and effort. Wish me luck.'

With a swift breath to concentrate her thoughts she bustled into the cubicle, hoping she was doing a passable impression of a harried junior doctor. With half of her brain absent without leave, wondering when Nick was going to make his appearance, it didn't take much acting.

'Nurse, why isn't this man undressed?' she demanded with a petulant edge to her voice as she followed Sally into the cubicle, her eyes cataloguing everything from the way he reacted to her sudden appearance and the size of his pupils to the colour of his skin and the way he forgot he was supposed to be guarding his painful stomach. 'I can't possibly examine him through all those clothes. Get them off him immediately. I can't send him up for an emergency operation and expect the theatre staff to take his clothes off.'

'But… He… You…' Sally floundered, clearly flustered by the unexpected direction the encounter was taking.

'Well, come on! Get to work with those scissors!' Libby chivvied. 'The man's in pain and we need to do something about it before he perforates and dies.'

'P-perforates?' the man in question repeated, trying to snatch his hand away from Libby's grasp when she approached him, pulling an IV drip stand into position with a bag of saline swinging wildly. She hoped she was giving every appearance of setting him up with a drip ready for transfer to Theatre. 'Perforates what? I only came in for some drugs…to take the pain away,' he added hastily. 'I don't need an operation.'

'Well, how would you know that?' Libby countered. 'Are you a doctor?'

'Well, no, but—'

'Have you had any tests to rule out a perforated bowel?' she interrupted again, making another grab for his hand.

'No!' he squawked, twisting out of her reach in a manoeuvre that would have caused him agony if he'd really been suffering from renal colic. 'All I need is—'

'Well, then,' she snapped officiously, not allowing him to continue. Now that she was almost certain that he wasn't really suffering from anything more than drugs withdrawal, there was no reason to go easy on him. 'Let the nurse cut your clothes off quickly and we can get on with our jobs. If you're in that much pain

I can't understand why you're causing such a fuss, especially when I'm putting you right at the head of the queue. The surgeon's waiting to start the incision as soon as you get up there. I can guarantee you won't have a problem with kidney stones again.'

With every word his agitation had increased and he had begun to resemble a cornered animal when he suddenly grew still, his eyes fixed on Libby's face.

'No! I'm not having any operation and you can't make me,' he declared belligerently. 'I know my rights.'

'Of course you don't have to have an operation if there's nothing wrong with you,' Libby agreed easily, before hardening her voice again. 'But you shouldn't be wasting our time either, trying to pull the wool over our eyes just so you can get a drugs fix. We see it happen far too often to be taken in by scam artists like you.'

With every moment she'd spent in the cubicle with him, the symptoms of his addiction had become more and more obvious. There had always been the chance that he was genuinely suffering from the agonising effects of trying to pass a kidney stone, but his sudden capitulation told her she'd definitely got it right this time.

'All right! So you saw through it,' he snarled, but there must have been something in her expression that made him think better of that attitude and he whined pathetically, 'But I haven't had a fix since yesterday, Doc. Can't you give me something just to tide me over?'

'You know very well that I can't do that—not without being struck off,' Libby said firmly. 'If you're a registered addict, you already know the system, and if not, the nurse will give you a leaflet with all the relevant information before you leave.'

'Bitch!' he spat as she exited the cubicle not quite certain whether to be cross at the waste of time or sorry at the waste of a life if her erstwhile patient carried on the way he was going.

'Not a lot of spare sympathy for your patients, then,' growled a voice right in her ear, and the unexpected surprise of it nearly sent her into orbit.

'Very little sympathy for people who voluntarily abuse their bodies and expect the rest of us to pay the costs and pick up the pieces,' she snapped, hoping Nick couldn't hear how breathless she was, or see how fast her pulse was beating with him looming over her that way. 'I reckon there'd be enough money to get rid of the operating waiting lists completely if we weren't having to spend so much money rescuing people from the effects of drink and drugs.'

To her surprise, he suddenly grinned, his blue eyes gleaming far too brightly under the glare of fluorescent lighting for her equilibrium. 'So, still no controversial opinions, then?' he teased, and she realised suddenly that he'd done it deliberately…provoked her into voicing her opinion.

'You used to do that when we were having a class discussion…at med school,' she said, as the forgotten memory suddenly leapt into full focus. It had been the only time when she'd been able to bear drawing attention to herself— for her knowledge and principles rather than her appearance or her wit—and she was surprised that he'd even remembered that about her when he'd had everyone else in the class hanging around him.

'Did I?' he said shortly, the humour erased from his face in the blink of an eye so that it was as though it had never existed. 'It was a long time ago.' And he was striding away down the wide corridor leaving Libby open-mouthed in his wake.

What on earth had she said wrong?

'So much for having a good working relationship with your boss,' she muttered under her breath as she made her way back to the whiteboard for her next assignment, knowing that only by keeping busy would she be able to stop herself thinking about the ache of disappointment that weighed her down.

For just those few seconds she'd actually known what it felt like to bask under Nick's smile. She'd actually been able to believe, just for a moment, that he was enjoying talking to her…teasing her. She should have known that real life couldn't possibly imitate all the heated fantasies she'd had about the golden boy of their class suddenly noticing the plump little brown mouse hiding in the corner and choosing her company above all the rest.

'Grow up!' she muttered under her breath. 'That was nothing more than a teenage crush. You're a grown woman now, and you've got Tash to take care of. No man's going to be interested in you—not with someone else's child in tow. You've missed the boat.'

But somehow it didn't seem to matter how logical and rational she tried to be. It certainly didn't seem to matter that she tried to tell herself that it had been nothing more than a belated teenage crush. All she knew was that the crazy corner of her heart that she'd lost the first time Nick had turned those gorgeous blue eyes on her still seemed to belong to him, even though he seemed destined to do nothing more than scowl at her.

But this was neither the time nor the place to think about that, not when the board was rapidly filling up with the next wave of patients needing their attention.

She didn't even reach the board before turning to follow an urgently beckoning staff nurse into a cubicle.

The young woman huddled on the examining couch was curled tightly into a foetal position, her whole body shuddering with tremors in spite of the blankets shrouding her. Her eyes were wide and staring and darkly dilated with shock and she seemed totally unaware of the fact that she was silently weeping.

'How far have you got? Have you done any obs? Do you know what happened?' Libby murmured softly, hoping to find out a few facts before she approached.

'We've got no details at all,' the young nurse began. 'She was found like this in the alley at the back of one of the rows of shops just off the town centre. One of the shopkeepers saw her when he was getting ready to open up this morning and phoned for an ambulance. At first, he thought she was just sleeping rough or on drugs or something, but…'

That had been Libby's initial assumption, too,

when she'd seen the dirty foot in tattered tights peeping out from the encompassing blankets. Then she realised that what she could see of the woman's hair was beautifully shiny and the solitary shoe that had come into the cubicle with her was good-quality leather and relatively new.

'So, have we got a name for her?' Libby approached the quivering bundle and bent over to have her first close look, only to be startled by the woman's convulsive jerk backwards in an obvious move to put more distance between the two of them.

'No ID at all,' said the quiet voice behind her, but Libby hardly needed the confirmation. Her stomach had given a sickening lurch when she recognised the traumatised response to her proximity.

'All right, sweetheart,' she crooned as she crouched down to place her own head lower than her patient's, knowing that would appear less threatening than looming over her. 'I promise I'm not going to do anything without warning you first and giving you a choice. OK?'

There wasn't even a flicker in the empty eyes to show that she'd even heard, let alone understood, but Libby had to persevere.

'Sweetheart, can you tell me where you hurt? Or can you show me?' she suggested. 'Are your feet bleeding? Can I just have a look to see if you got any cuts on them?' She paused a moment, half expecting a refusal, then, when nothing happened, took it as tacit agreement and reached out to lift the bottom edge of the blanket.

As she'd expected, one foot was completely unscathed but the other had several minor puncture wounds that were bleeding sluggishly through the layer of grime that coated them.

'Can I clean these up a bit?' she asked, stroking a gentle finger under the slender arch. As she'd hoped, this time there was a reaction. The foot was swiftly withdrawn even as its owner stifled a sound. 'Aha! You're ticklish!' Libby declared gleefully, and with a leap of relief she found herself making genuine eye contact with her patient for the first time.

It was only a minor breakthrough but it was

definitely something she could build on in her need to form a bond of trust between the two of them. The trouble was, that was something that could take time, and with more and more patients arriving in the department, time was something in short supply.

'Lucy, can you let Sister know that I could be some time?' she said softly to the hovering nurse. Even though events were more than eight years in the past, she could empathise only too well with what the traumatised woman was going through and was determined not to abandon her now that she'd made a connection. 'Obviously, she'll call me if everything hits the fan out there, but...'

'I'll tell her,' Lucy said, equally quietly. 'Just stick your head out through the curtains and shout if you need me back.'

It took nearly an hour of patience and soft conversation—mostly one-sided—to coax Gillian Marsh into giving her details, and even longer before she consented to an examination, but by the time her injuries had been catalogued and treated she had told Libby about the neatly dressed young man who had stopped her to ask for directions and had ended up dragging her into a nearby alley to steal everything she had been carrying.

'At first, I thought he was going to rape me and I was so shocked that I didn't know what to do,' Gillian said with a sound halfway between a laugh and a sob as Libby used glue to repair the laceration in her scalp. 'I know the police tell you not to fight but…well, when I realised that he was trying to take my laptop and… I'd got all my work on it—weeks of it all ready for a presentation that… Oh, damn! I should be there now!' she wailed, and her eyes welled with tears for the first time. 'Now I'll lose the contract and my business will fold.'

'Not necessarily,' Libby said calmly as she stripped off her gloves. 'Surely, if the company realises you were unavoidably detained…?' She stopped when Gillian shook her head and saw her wince at the resulting ache.

'I'm just a minnow trying to play with

sharks,' she admitted sombrely as Libby filled in the forms that would accompany the young woman up to the X-ray department. There was a vicious bruise on one side of her ribs that looked like the result of a kick and she wanted to rule out the possibility of cracked ribs. The bruising on her hand was so clearly defined that she knew it had been stamped on at some stage.

'This was my last chance to go it alone,' Gillian continued, now seeming to need to tell her tale of woe. 'I'd actually managed to get an appointment to speak to the big chief of Cardew's—a really big PR job, almost a total rebranding of the company, since his father's retired. Now, I've blown it completely. I'll never get another chance like that, so I may as well cut my losses and start job-hunting...'

She had grown so silent by the time she set off to have her X-rays taken that Libby's heart went out to her.

With a 'See you when you get back after your X-rays' she was on her way to the board to check who was next in line for attention when an idea suddenly popped into her head.

'Kelly, have you got anything urgent for me, or can I use your office for a moment? I need to contact someone about Gillian Marsh...the mugging patient.'

'There's a queue as usual, but nothing desperate for a couple of minutes. Anything I can do?'

'No. It shouldn't take long...if I can get through. It would probably take longer to give you the details to pass on,' Libby said obliquely, not wanting to have to admit that this was one call she really wanted to make herself. Added to that, she wasn't absolutely certain that the department's most senior nurse would approve of what she intended to do.

In the event, it was all surprisingly easy and within five minutes she had a piece of paper burning a hole in her pocket while she waited for Gillian to return for the results of her X-rays.

'So, what's the verdict?' her subdued patient asked, barely interested enough to glance in their direction as Libby slipped the newly developed plates under the retaining clips on the light-boxes, her depression apparently growing by the minute.

In spite of her impatience, Libby was careful to take her time examining the plates. Missing a fracture had the potential to be life-threatening, especially if it resulted in a punctured lung.

'It's all good news,' she announced as she turned part way to direct Gillian's attention to the shadowy images. 'As far as we can tell, you haven't even cracked anything, so it's just a matter of waiting for the bruises to heal. Having said that, if you're unhappy with anything—if the pain gets worse, or sharper, come straight back, especially if you have any difficulty breathing or problems focusing.'

'So I haven't even got the excuse of broken bones to blame my failure on,' Gillian said morosely, her shoulders slumped as far as her bruised ribs would allow.

'Here's a piece of paper telling you what to look out for with your rib injuries and another about your head injury,' Libby continued, then added a third. 'And this last one is the most important. Whatever you do, don't lose it because it's the private number of Ian Cardew and he's waiting for you to ring him to set up another appointment.'

'He's…what?' Gillian's head whipped round towards her so fast that it must have hurt her aching head but she didn't even seem to notice it. '*What* did you say?' she demanded, now staring down at the slip of paper in Libby's hand as though afraid to blink in case it disappeared.

'I hope you don't mind my interference, but I thought he ought to know what had happened to you in case he was worried,' Libby explained, quite certain that her patient was probably only taking in one word in ten. 'I got his secretary to put me through—'

'You got past the dragon!' Gillian exclaimed wryly. 'Tell me your secret. It took me weeks.'

'Sometimes it's useful to be able to hide behind a title,' Libby said with a grin. 'Even overprotective secretaries balk at demanding your business with their boss.'

'So, what did you say…what did *he* say?'

she demanded, suddenly animated out of all recognition.

'Obviously, I couldn't break patient confidentiality, but I told him that the reason why you hadn't arrived for your appointment with him was that you'd been mugged and beaten and your injuries were being investigated in A and E. I told him that you were agitated that he might think you had deliberately let him down without warning.'

'*And?*' she prompted impatiently.

'And...he gave me his mobile phone number so you wouldn't have to go through the dragon—his father's choice of secretary, by the way—and said to tell you to phone him as soon as you escape from my clutches to tell him how you are and to set up another meeting.'

'Fantastic! Oh, that's just so... Oh, *no*! My laptop! It's gone, and everything on it for the presentation.'

'And you didn't bother keeping any notes or back-up copies of what you were working on?' Libby asked, now wondering if she'd only prolonged Gillian's misery. 'Was the only copy of everything in the laptop?'

'The polished presentation was,' Gillian admitted, but her mood was lightening by the second as her brain started to function again. 'But I've probably got dozens of copies of the various stages as I was working on it on my old computer.'

'So?' Libby prompted, willing her to take the next step.

'So, how long would it take to polish one of them up? Definitely a lot less time than starting from the beginning,' she admitted.

'So, that's what you tell the man when you phone him in five minutes' time,' Libby said with a wide smile as she helped her cautious patient into her scuffed coat without jarring her bruised ribs. 'And good luck!'

'I'll let you know how it goes,' Gillian said over her shoulder as she preceded Libby out of the room, not realising that the sight of the man she passed on her way down the corridor was the only one guaranteed to make Libby's heart miss a beat, even when he was frowning at her and glancing pointedly at the number of patients still waiting for attention.

CHAPTER THREE

'*SOCIAL WORKER!*' Libby muttered under her breath on her way to her next patient waiting in one of the curtained cubicles, unable to count the number of times she'd repeated the taunt to herself in the last couple of days.

That was what Nick had called her after Gillian Marsh had left to make her phone call and the accusation had stung, just as he had probably intended.

Not that she saw anything wrong with what she'd done for her patient, especially when Gillian had just called the department an hour ago to let Libby know that she had made her delayed presentation that morning and that she was in with a good chance of getting the job she'd wanted after all.

There had been a hefty dollop of satisfaction that her meddling had resulted in such a positive outcome even though it had absolutely nothing to do with her patient's injuries.

If only she could forget the way Nick had called her to task for going outside her remit as an A and E doctor...or, more specifically, if only she could ignore the fact that it seemed to matter more and more that he should think well of her and her skills as a doctor.

'Oh, no! Not a bird!' groaned her latest patient when she entered the cubicle and drew the curtain across behind her.

'I beg your pardon?' Libby wasn't certain she'd heard the young man right. It was usually the older, more conservative men who had difficulty coping with women doctors, not the younger ones. They had more of a tendency to use it as an opportunity to make suggestive remarks.

'No offence, Doctor!' he said hastily, probably goaded into a weak excuse of an apology by the fierce expression on her face. His own looked decidedly green against the paper covering the pillow behind his head, and the fresh disposable bowl beside him clearly wasn't the first he'd needed. 'But I really need to see a man.'

'It may come as a surprise to you, Simon, but we get exactly the same training whether we're male or female,' Libby said patiently, using the delay to scan the brief details on his case notes and cast a keen eye over the way he was curled up on his side and the pained expression on his face when he unconsciously moved his legs. 'I'm unlikely to be shocked by anything you tell me, from piercings gone wrong to sexually transmitted diseases to over-enthusiastic homosexual encounters…' She deliberately conjured up some of the more colourful cases she'd heard about from other A and E staff, even though she hadn't come across all of them herself…yet.

'God, no! It's nothing like that,' he gasped, his scarlet face evidence of his relative innocence. 'I was playing football with me mates and just got kicked in my…' He gestured down towards his genitalia.

'And you want to be sure there hasn't been

any permanent damage to the family jewels?' Libby finished for him, reaching for a fresh pair of gloves. 'Well, in that case, the sooner we start, the sooner you'll know.'

Simon threw a last despairing look towards the curtains, as though contemplating making a run for it. For just a moment Libby contemplated finding out if Nick was free to spare her patient's blushes—even though she knew it would be something else he could use against her—but then the young man sighed heavily and allowed the nurse to pull his covering away.

'That's an impressive bruise,' Libby commented as she stepped closer, hoping she'd managed to suppress her wince at the thought of the degree of pain he must have been in. 'And there's a large amount of swelling, too.'

'Oh, that's not just from the kick,' Simon interrupted, dragging his eyes away from the ceiling to look at her for the first time since he'd been exposed to public gaze. 'One of them's been bigger than the other for…well, some time now.'

Libby's antennae tingled. 'How long? Weeks?

Months?' Suddenly, this was becoming more serious by the moment. A stray kick in the wrong place could do enough damage to permanently stop the affected testicle from functioning, but now it seemed that there had been something going on even before his current injury.

'Several months,' he admitted. 'Four or five, perhaps, but I'm not sure because I don't...you know...play with myself like that. But recently it's been getting bigger and starting to hurt—not as bad as this, though.'

Alarm bells were now sounding loudly in her head, especially since she'd examined him. She knew that most lumps in that area weren't caused by testicular cancer but this was definitely a solid lump in a testis and probably was, especially given his age and his description of his symptoms. What an ultrasound scan wouldn't be able to tell her was which of the four types of cancer was involved, so she had no idea whether he had a ninety-six per cent chance of long-term survival or just a matter of months.

'With your permission, I'd like to do an ultrasound scan to see exactly what sort of damage there is in there, and I'd like to take some blood for screening,' Libby explained briefly. 'Then, as soon as we get the results, I'll get the doctor who specialises in this sort of thing to tell you what we've found—and this time I can promise you it will be a man!'

He smiled wryly. 'So, how long will I have to wait for that? Will I get an appointment to tell me when to come back and some painkillers in the meantime?'

'Oh, no. Because of the possibility that you've got some damaged blood vessels in there, we'll do it all today,' she said brightly, glad that he didn't know her well enough to know that she was holding back on the devastating possibilities. 'You'll have all the answers before you go home.'

She managed to smile right up to the moment when she drew the curtain behind her, leaving Judy to draw blood to determine the tell-tale levels of alpha-fetoprotein and human chorionic gonadotrophin.

Unfortunately, the fierce frown that descended as she concentrated on sorting out who she should contact first to get Simon's investigation under way coincided with coming face to face with Nick.

'A genuine medical problem this time?' he queried, and she nearly snapped at him for the taunt. Only the fact that he was effectively her boss on this shift and that she needed to ask his advice to get the speediest diagnosis and treatment for Simon stilled her tongue long enough to choose her words wisely.

'Who would you recommend to do a biopsy on a query testicular cancer and how quickly can we get it done?' she demanded briskly once they were out of earshot of the patient in question. 'I've organised bloods and the ultrasound tech will be here as soon as she can, but the situation's been complicated by a recent kick during a football game.'

His wince was a predictably sympathetic male response. 'Doug Andrews,' he said without hesitation. 'That's who I'd want if it were me. Would you like me to give him a buzz and see how soon he could squeeze it in?'

For a second her pride was piqued that he might be suggesting she couldn't organise it herself but then logic told her that Simon's needs were more important than her ego, even where Nick was concerned.

'Would you?' She grabbed the ubiquitous pad of paper from her pocket, a free gift from one of the drugs companies emblazoned with an advert for the latest wonder cure, and jotted down Simon's basic details. 'He's staying in curtains for the moment. I'm going to grab something to drink, but as soon as you know anything, give me a shout and I'll—'

'Libby…phone!' called a voice from the main reception desk as Nick started to stride away, and she ignored the sharp look he threw at her over his shoulder as she made her way to the increased privacy of the staff lounge. If he thought it was her busy social life intruding on her job, he couldn't be more mistaken, she thought as she reached for the instrument. She had no idea who might be calling her. Since she'd moved to St Luke's, she'd barely had time to get to know her colleagues at work, let alone get to know anyone who might phone her from outside the hospital.

'Libby Cornish,' she announced into the handset, stifling a sigh of relief as she perched on the arm of a nearby chair to take the weight off her feet.

'Mrs Cornish?' asked the disembodied voice in her ear.

'Dr Cornish,' she corrected automatically, grateful as ever for the unisex title that gave no indication of her marital status. 'How can I help you?'

If this was a telephone pitch to get her to buy double glazing or to give away a free holiday if she'd sign up for a dodgy time-share apartment…

'Oh, I didn't realise… Oh, dear…well…' The idea that she was a doctor seemed to have thoroughly flustered the woman on the other end. 'My name is Mrs Judy Peverill…and I'm Natasha's teacher—we met when you enrolled her and when you brought her to school on her first day.'

That was enough to get her instant concentration. Her stomach had never travelled from her throat to her boots so fast before.

'Tash? What's the matter with Tash?' She didn't know whether to hope that her daughter was in disgrace for an infraction of school rules or that she'd had some minor mishap in the playground.

'I really don't think it's anything to worry about,' the voice said bracingly, 'but your daughter has had a nosebleed and we don't seem to be able to get it to stop so we thought she ought to come to the hospital. One of the classroom assistants is bringing her by car.'

'Thank you for letting me know,' Libby said quickly when it seemed as if the woman was going to go into further details. All she was interested in was getting to the reception desk to be there when Tash came through the doors. She could only imagine how scared she must be, in spite of the fact that it was the place where her mother worked.

Blind and deaf to everything else, Libby hurried out of the room and promptly ploughed into the solid figure who had been about to push the door open.

'Libby,' Nick began with a frown, but she didn't have time to waste finding out what he was coming to find her for, even if it was news about Simon.

'Sorry! Can't stop,' she called over her shoulder, and lengthened her stride to something just short of running in her eagerness. 'There's a patient coming in.'

She was only just in time as the department's main reception doors swished open to reveal a very miserable little girl clutching a large handful of blood-soaked tissues to her nose.

'Tash! Sweetheart, what happened?' Libby demanded, dropping to her knees to gather her precious child into her arms, totally unconcerned that she would have to change her stained clothing again. 'Did you have a fight with somebody? Did they hit you in the face?'

'We don't think there was any fight, Mrs Corn—Dr Cornish,' the middle-aged classroom assistant corrected herself swiftly after a glance at Libby's name tag. 'The bleeding actually started while they were sitting in the classroom during story time.'

Libby stood up, cradling Tash in her arms as she rose and grateful that she could still do it. The day couldn't be too far off when her slender daughter would be too tall and too heavy to carry, but today, when her child was hurt, it was reassuring for both of them to give her the comfort of a cuddle.

'We tried putting ice cubes on the bridge of her nose and pinching it, like I did for my own children, but nothing seemed to work,' the woman said as she followed Libby into the first free treatment room, clearly upset by her failure. 'The headmistress thought it would be a good idea to bring her here because it was distressing the other children. We hadn't realised that you actually worked here, in the accident department.'

'It was all in the contact information I filled in when I registered her at the school, with the phone number,' Libby said distractedly, aware that Tash was far too quiet and growing paler by the minute. 'Look, I'm not being rude, but I'm going to take Tash through to see why the bleeding isn't stopping. Thank you for bringing her in to the hospital for me.' And she walked away at a rapid pace towards the nearest treatment room, the classroom assistant completely dismissed from her mind. The only thing that mattered was taking care of her precious child.

'What's going on?' Nick demanded when he followed her into the brightly lit room seconds later, almost as if he'd been waiting for her to arrive. 'Who brought this child in? A parent? A teacher? She's far too young to be here on her own.'

'*I'm* her parent,' Libby declared distractedly, more concerned with the fact that Tash was beginning to look decidedly shocky. Could she really have lost that much blood? 'Tash is my daughter.'

'Mum...I feel sick,' the little girl whimpered, and proceeded to vomit the blood-stained contents of her stomach.

Nick was barely conscious that he'd automatically reached for a basin, or that he'd positioned it in exactly the right place to prevent Libby's shoulder being decorated with the result. There was only one thing that he could think about as he helped Libby position the child on the couch so that the blood didn't trickle down her throat into her stomach. One thing filled his head to the exclusion of everything else—this was *Libby's* child.

He felt as shocked as if he'd been hit over the head with a blunt object...or was it his heart? The pain around it felt almost as if a giant hand was squeezing it mercilessly, stopping it from beating properly.

How could she? he railed silently as he took over from her trembling efforts to set up an IV. *She'd obviously just calmly got on with her life as though...*

'We need to get some astringent and packing into her nose to get that bleeding stopped,' Nick muttered, deliberately switching off the voice inside his head. The overwhelming feeling of betrayal that had gripped him was something he would have to deal with later. For now, they had a little patient bleeding copiously and the child's mother who looked as if she was going to pass out at any minute. 'Go and get someone else in here to deal with it,' he ordered, only just tempering his anger towards Libby in time to prevent himself frightening her daughter. 'You shouldn't be treating your own family.'

'I'm not leaving her,' Libby declared bluntly, defiance blazing out at him from those unfor-gettable blue-green eyes...eyes that exactly matched the younger version on the couch. 'I'm all she's got.'

Nick felt a totally illogical blaze of satisfac-tion roar through him at those words and knew that he was going to have to wait until later to examine that, too. But he couldn't stop himself from speculating.

Was it proof that the child's father was no longer in the picture? And why should it matter to him, anyway? He certainly didn't want to have anything to do with Libby Cornish.

In the meantime, there was a little girl relying on him to treat her and a woman with all the protective instincts of a mother lion watching his every move.

In the event, it took almost no time at all to stem the bleeding and before the unit of replacement fluids had finished dripping down through the IV, the little sprite was already running Libby ragged with non-stop questions about everything that was going on around her.

Nick found himself fascinated.

For someone who looked so much like Libby, it was amazing just how different they were. Where the young Libby he'd first known had been quiet and self-effacing, her daughter didn't seem to have a shy bone in her body and approached everything—even her own current circumstances—with curiosity and boundless enthusiasm.

'Enough!' Libby exclaimed, when Tash seemed as if she was going to ask for a detailed account of every item of equipment in the room. 'You're supposed to be staying quiet to give your body a chance to recover.'

'I'm fine, Mum. Great. And I'm starving,' she announced, clearly raring to get on with her life. 'Can we go and get some fish and chips on the way home?'

Nick saw the moment Libby realised the dilemma of every working mother...the need to be with her child warring with her responsibility to her profession.

'Who usually takes care of her when you're on duty?' he asked, strangely reluctant to leave her to resolve the problem alone.

'One of the other mums takes her home from school with her own daughter, Mia. We live within walking distance of each other and Layla's a classroom assistant at their school.'

'And if she's unavailable? What's your back-up plan?'

'I haven't needed one before,' she admitted, worrying her lip with anxious teeth. 'Tash hasn't had anything more than grazed knees or a cold since she first started school and we've only lived here a few months...not long enough to build up a big circle of friends.'

'So you'd better go and get yourself changed into your street clothes so you can take her home,' he suggested. 'She's bounced back very fast, but it would be better if she took it gently for the rest of the day, at least.'

'But I can't just leave!' Libby objected, clearly horrified. 'I'm on duty until six.'

'Well, that leaves us with the alternative of admitting your daughter to the ward, which seems a little excessive for a nosebleed.'

'But...' She was clearly torn.

'Oh, for heaven's sake!' he exclaimed. 'Your concentration would be shot for the rest of the day anyway. You may as well go home, for all the good you'll do. I'll go and see if there's anyone we can pull in early to cover the rest of your shift. You can make up your time later, or take it as part of your holiday entitlement.'

He left the two of them slightly open-mouthed as he left the room and was surprised to feel the burn of a blush in his cheeks. That was the least of his worries, though. What was of more concern and the reason why he'd been so abrupt was the crazy feeling that had come over him that he'd wanted to get personally involved with Libby and her problems, and that was something he never did. Not for anyone. Not any more. Not since…

'Enough!' he growled, and cut off the thought. Libby was just another member of staff with a temporary need to take care of her child in the middle of a shift. He'd made the only sensible suggestion and that was the end of the matter. He definitely wasn't going to be spending a single minute wondering where the two of them lived or how they would spend the rest of the day with Libby trying to keep her livewire daughter still.

And he definitely wasn't going to be wasting a single second feeling anger and regret at the fact that bright sparky Tash was the child he would never have, a child he would have loved to call his own.

Rationally, he could tell himself that the only reason why he felt protective towards her was because it was part of his profession to care. He certainly didn't want to have children, not any more, because that would mean having a relationship and that meant risking having your heart torn out by the roots and shredded, and he wasn't going to go through that sort of pain again, not while he had a single functioning brain cell.

And the last thing he was going to think about was the identity of the man who had fathered Libby's daughter because that would mean thinking about the intimacies that would have been involved in her conception and that would mean he had to admit that, even though it had been ripped out by the roots, his heart could still ache with the pain of rejection.

'Mum? Am I going to school today?'

Libby slowly surfaced from her dream to her daughter's voice, but the images still lingered long enough in her brain to tell her that it was the same dream that had been returning night after night since she'd realised she would be working with Nick Howell.

'Mum? Am I?' Tash persisted, her voice comically nasal in tone due to the packing that was going to be removed that morning.

'I'll tell you when I've seen to your nose, but probably, yes,' she mumbled, still trying to hold onto the elusive images that were fading with her return to consciousness.

What did the dream mean?

Why was she always standing in the dark, in the rain, without an umbrella, soaking wet. And why did Kolya...? *Nick*, she corrected herself angrily, still uncertain why her sleep-fogged brain had readily conjured up that strange nick-name. Why did Nick appear beside her in her dream, dry underneath his huge umbrella and offering to shelter her?

It wasn't too hard to interpret the images in a way that suggested her subconscious saw the man as a strong, caring, protective person, especially when her life was filled with the stress of single parenthood. After all, doctors, and especially A and E doctors, were the ultimate alpha males that women were genetically pro-grammed to seek for their protective strength.

So, why did she have the feeling that there was something far more significant in the recurring images? Why was it that the scene always seemed to start in exactly the same way but each time apparently continued just that little bit longer with just that bit more detail?

This morning had been no different, in spite of the fact that Tash had woken her so early. This time, Nick hadn't just offered her a space under his umbrella but had slid an arm around her shoulders to pull her close to him, his head bending towards her as though...

No! That was just leftover wishful thinking from when she'd had her juvenile crush on the man when they'd been students together. She couldn't possibly be spending her nights dreaming about kissing the man...could she?

'How is Tash today?' Nick asked before Libby had even managed to get her coat off. 'Has she gone back to school?'

'Yes. She was desperate to go so she could tell her friends all about the hospital. She's as bright and chirpy as though it had never happened,' Libby replied, her relief at the happy outcome suddenly mixed with a crazy measure of embarrassment, as though Nick might somehow know about her recurring dream and his role in it.

'It never ceases to amaze me just how resilient children are,' he said, with what was probably the first totally spontaneous smile he'd aimed in her direction since he'd realised they'd be working together.

When she'd known him before, he'd been a man who'd smiled easily, but all she'd seen had been frowns and scowls directed at her. This lighter mood was enough to set her pulse tripping into double time.

'Oh, by the way,' he added, 'I didn't have time to say anything before you left yesterday, but that was a neat bit of diagnosis on the lad with testicular cancer.'

'So it *was* cancer.' Knowing the sort of treatment that the young man was going to have to go through, she was upset for him, but felt a warm glow of satisfaction that she'd asked all the right questions to pick up on the disease.

'Doug Andrews stayed late and operated yesterday evening, tacking him onto the end of his list,' Nick went on. 'He said—and I quote—"To hell with the hospital management's stupid arbitrary budgets and performance targets, this needs to come out *now*." Oh, and he sent his compliments on your good instincts,' he added as he reached the door. 'He's hopeful that it's been caught before it had a chance to spread.'

So, why did Nick's approval matter more to her than that of the top oncologist in the hospital? she wondered a few minutes later as she cupped her rapidly cooling mug of coffee in both hands.

Was it because it had been so hard to please him since she'd come here, or was it just because of the simple pleasure of having the wretched man smile at her at last?

'You're pathetic!' she muttered under her breath as she got up to tip the rest of the coffee away. 'Just as pathetic as you were when you used to follow him everywhere with your eyes, watching him chatting up every female in sight and hurt because it was never your turn.'

'That bad, eh?' said a deep voice beside her, and she nearly leapt out of her skin. She hadn't even noticed anyone walking towards her, let alone realised that there was someone close enough to hear her talking to herself. How much had he heard? Enough to put two and two together? Enough to gossip about?

Grimly, she forced herself to turn and face the man and found herself looking up into the smiling face of David ffrench.

'It's Libby, isn't it? You came up last week to see the baby we had to deliver in A and E…the emergency Caesarean. I told you then that this place would get to you,' he chided jokingly. 'You should have taken my advice and changed your specialty. We're much more civilised up on Obs and Gyn.'

His teasing should have been just what she needed to snap her out of her thoughts, but there was another tension entirely wrapping itself around her throat now that he was standing here chatting to her. More secrets that she was having to keep to herself because she didn't know how far the ripples would spread…how much damage it would do if she told him…

'Look, is everything all right?' he asked solicitously. 'You look a bit…out of it. Shall I make you a fresh coffee?'

The cowardly part of her wanted to run a mile but the more rational side welcomed the unexpected chance to get to know the man better. There wouldn't be very many opportunities to sit and chat to him without the world looking on, not without looking as if she was chasing after the man and risking making people suspicious of her motives.

'Yes, thank you. That would be—'

'Libby. RTA coming in.' Nick's voice cracked across the room like a whip and there was no sign of a smile now. 'No time for second cups of coffee in our department…unlike the leisurely life up in Obs and Gyn,' he added pointedly for David's benefit, but as he held the door open for her Libby could see that the polite smile he'd pasted on his face for his senior colleague certainly didn't reach his eyes.

It was almost as if he wanted to make sure she didn't linger with David, she thought as she followed him out into the wide corridor, although why...

'You do know he's married, don't you?' Nick said as soon as the door closed behind them, preventing David from hearing what he said. 'And very happily married, too, so there's no point setting your cap at him.' And before she could catch her breath from the shock of the implied accusation he was striding away towards the other end of the department and the rising crescendo of ambulance sirens.

CHAPTER FOUR

THERE were injuries ranging from a painfully wrenched thumb to life-threatening fractured cervical vertebrae to be dealt with in the next four hours and throughout them, Libby seethed.

She was stunned that Nick could think she would do something as underhand as make a play for another woman's husband. What right did he have to judge her like that? She wasn't the only single mother in the department and none of the others seemed to come under the same barrage of black looks as she did.

'I know it's uncomfortable, but you know that the cervical collar has to stay put until the orthopaedic consultant has had a look at your X-rays,' she reminded the young medical student with the fractured vertebrae. She would leave it up to the head of orthopaedics to break the news that he was probably going to have to have a metal frame installed to stabilise his neck until everything healed.

Heaven only knew how far back that would set his training as a doctor, or if he was ever going to be able to return to it. So far, everything had gone right for him in that his neck had been swiftly immobilised at the site of the crash before he had been laboriously cut out of his vehicle *and* before any neurological damage had been done. Even so, she had no idea how much effect his injuries would have on him in the future, especially if his neck had to be permanently immobilised to prevent paralysis.

She breathed a sigh of relief as the lift doors closed behind him on his way up to be admitted to the orthopaedic ward and the start of the long road to recovery, glad that everything that had been done in the A and E department had helped towards that result. She'd really had to concentrate, second-guessing every one of her own moves to make certain she wasn't missing anything or doing further, irreparable damage. She wouldn't be able to live with herself if her angry thoughts towards Nick had compromised her patient's health.

That didn't mean she wasn't still furious with him, but in the long run, what did he care about that fury? She was the only one who was suffering for it with compromised attention, so it had to stop.

'I've got to put the blasted man out of my mind until I've got a chance to tell him what I think of him and his insinuations,' she muttered to herself as she stood in front of the board again to check up on the status of the patients waiting for attention.

'You're talking to yourself again,' Sally teased as she reached up to wipe another name off, signifying that another body had either been treated and sent home, or admitted to the appropriate ward. 'Sounds like you need a break.'

For the first time in hours there were actually some gaps on the board, indicating empty cubicles and treatment rooms, and there were no serious injuries waiting for attention at all.

'I think you're right,' Libby agreed, glad that Sally hadn't heard what she'd said. She'd have to be more careful. The last thing she wanted was to provide the gossip grapevine with any juicy titbits. 'If the time on that clock is correct, I've been working without a break for four hours.'

'In that case, the patients waiting for attention to minor injuries will just have to wait a little longer while you get a hot drink into yourself,' Sally said firmly. 'A meal break might have to wait a little longer, but you're going to become dehydrated if you carry on like this. Then your brain won't function properly.'

'Are you sure you've got enough staff on? I must admit, I'm gasping for some tea,' Libby admitted. She was also more tired than she'd realised, having slept far more lightly than usual with one ear trained on Tash.

Was it this way for other medical personnel with children? she wondered as she took her first sip of the steaming brew. Did they spend their time trying not to imagine that every sniffle and bump was the first sign of a life-threatening disease? Or did they over-compensate by dismissing real symptoms in an attempt not to seem paranoid and over-protective?

Life had definitely been easier when her mother had been around to talk to. Her down-to-earth, non-medical perspective had been the perfect balance for Libby's over-active imagination and, in the absence of a 'significant other', she had been a sorely needed confidante.

'Are you sure you're coping?' demanded a voice just behind her, and the shock of Nick's unexpected presence made her jerk so hard that she nearly sent her tea into orbit. 'Wouldn't it be better if you did something less stressful than A and E?' he continued as she recognised her heart's usual crazy leap in her chest, and her temper shot up like a ballistic missile.

'I am coping perfectly well, thank you,' she said icily, determined not to feel at a disadvantage even though he was towering in front of her and preventing her from getting to her feet. 'Unless you've had any complaints?'

'No complaints at all,' he responded seriously. 'But I was surprised to see you at work today. I thought you would have stayed home with your daughter.'

'I would have, if she was at home,' she said honestly, even as she felt a renewed pang of guilt that she'd been relieved Tash didn't need her to miss another shift. 'I may not have had a back-up plan organised yesterday, but that was just because Tash hasn't been ill since my mother died. Today, I would have had to handcuff her to her bed to stop her going in to play with her new friends. She may not be back up to full bounce but she was desperate to get back to school.'

'Well, *she* may be full of bounce, but *you* look as white as a sheet,' he accused, and the way his keen eyes scanned her sleep-deprived face was anything but the caressing gaze she'd fantasised about. Not that her pulse rate seemed to recognise the difference, dammit.

'The fact that I occasionally need to stop for

refreshment only goes to prove that I'm not a robot,' she snapped back, and was surprised to see one corner of his mouth twitch as though he was fighting the urge to smile. Unfortunately, that little quirk—one that had appeared many times when he'd been confronted by a humorous situation during their training—was just as attractive as ever and as her anger melted away she realised that she still found it impossible to resist.

'Neither R2D2 nor C3PO,' he agreed seriously, just before the grin finally broke through.

That smile! It had haunted her ever since her first day at medical school and was every bit as potent now. Then, she would have given anything to have him direct it towards her, or even to have him notice her sitting studiously in her self-imposed isolation. Now...

'Just make certain you stop to eat, too,' he admonished, suddenly serious again. 'We don't want you keeling over. It would be very bad publicity for the department.'

What *was* it about the woman that got to him?

Nick was still brooding over his response to

Libby at the end of his shift. He still couldn't believe the clumsy way he'd put her back up, but when he'd seen her sitting there, cradling that steaming mug of tea as though chilled to the bone and so dejected-looking…

'Protective?' he mused aloud, and gave a brief bark of laughter. Once upon a time he'd felt far more than protective towards quiet, shy Libby Cornish, for all the good it had done him. He'd actually believed that she…

'Enough! Been there, done that and didn't enjoy it the first time around,' he reminded himself, needing to hear the words spoken aloud. Then he had to silently admit that he wasn't being strictly honest with himself. There had been that glorious week, almost exactly halfway through their medical training, when the two of them had finally stopped circling around each other.

After years of focusing on his goal of becoming a doctor—to the exclusion of almost everything else—the sense of connection he'd felt when he'd looked down into her eyes had been a revelation to him.

Oh, he'd been popular enough, he couldn't deny that. Without being big-headed, he could say that there had always been plenty of pretty girls smiling at him. But that was more a case of the lucky combination of genes that had given him his looks and the fact that he genuinely enjoyed meeting people. He'd tried to be on friendly terms with the female half of his year, even the shy, slightly plump one who'd seemed to avoid so much as meeting his eyes, but he definitely hadn't wanted to get involved in a relationship because he had been certain he couldn't spare the time.

Until the evening he'd been slogging his way back towards his bedsit through torrential rain, his umbrella doing little to keep anything but his head and shoulders dry, when he'd seen a couple of youngsters dart across the road and snatch the umbrella from the young woman in front of him.

They'd jostled her so roughly that she'd reeled

against the wall beside her and almost fallen by the time he reached her.

'Are you all right?' he demanded, one arm wrapped securely around her shoulders to steady her on her feet. Then she looked up at him and he realised it was Libby, her fascinating blue-green eyes wide with shock and framed by dark hair already dripping with rain, and with a strange feeling of inevitability, he was lost.

Their first kiss told him everything he needed to know—that timing didn't matter when you found the person who was meant to share the rest of your life.

'My single brain cell moved south, more likely,' he growled, still feeling ashamed of the way he'd completely fallen apart when she'd simply disappeared a few weeks later.

He'd been out of control, frantic to know what had happened to her. For the first time his career hadn't been the be-all and end-all of his existence, and when he'd discovered that she'd just gone away without a word…well, he'd been so devastated that if it hadn't been for his tutor's persistence he might never have got back on track.

'Well, it won't be happening again,' he reminded himself with a determined nod. 'It doesn't matter if she does still press some of the old buttons. That's just a knee-jerk response or a hormonal reaction. I'm not fool enough to think it means anything to her, not after the last time.'

It had been the only time he'd ever become deeply involved, a fact that angered him all over again now that he realised that he'd virtually allowed his life to stand still since Libby had walked out of it. When he looked back he could see that he'd seldom dated any woman for more than a few weeks and had sometimes gone months between dates. 'While she carried blithely on with her life with hardly a hiccup, collecting her qualification and a child along the way.'

The bitterness that echoed around his bedroom brought him up sharply, making him realise that if he was going to get any sleep he was going to have to sort his head out, and quickly.

Was *that* what it was all about, this renewed

animosity he felt towards Libby? Was it just because he still felt as if she'd played him for a fool or had it been a far deeper emotion? Was he being so hard on her for a petty reason that he should have forgotten years ago or had the damage she'd done formed scars that had left him permanently emotionally disabled?

It seemed only fitting that it was his childhood bedroom that should be the venue for what felt like decidedly adolescent heart-searching. With his parents away on their once-in-a-lifetime trip, he was dividing his off-duty time between their house and his own flat, so it could even be these old surroundings that had triggered this introspective mood.

The trouble was, it didn't seem to matter how determined he was not to let Libby get under his skin. She obviously wasn't the sort of inoculation that conferred lifelong immunity because, in spite of his animosity, he felt just as attracted to her as ever.

'That's not to say that I'd ever fall in love with her…or anyone…again,' he declared aloud into the darkness, then wondered why he seemed to hear hollow laughter inside his head as he finally drifted off to sleep.

He'd kissed her! Nick Howell had kissed her, she exulted, her heart pounding in her chest.

Then Libby tried to roll over and found the other half of her bed firmly occupied by her daughter's generously splayed form and realisation dawned.

It had only been a dream…*the* dream…but it had seemed so real when he'd finally bent his head to touch his lips to hers that she was absolutely certain that she knew how it would feel in real life.

'As if!' she whispered softly, cursing her over-active imagination and the fact that working with the man seemed to have resurrected all her old fantasies…except there was something strange about the way this one had ended.

Even as it had been going on inside her head it had seemed far too real to be nothing more than a dream, even though it had started in exactly the same way as the others. She lay very still and let her mind drift back, hoping to recall every shred of information, frustrating though it might be.

This time, she had been pursued by someone or something and her heartbeat had soared with the sudden recognition of danger. There had been a struggle and then she'd been deluged with icy water and left feeling vulnerable and exposed until, from nowhere, someone had appeared to shelter her with his umbrella.

She remembered looking up into Nick's face and the sudden heart-stopping realisation that he was leaning closer with a purposeful look on his face. And then his lips had met hers with a potent mixture of gentleness and hunger that had made her heart soar, and she'd suddenly known that this was what she had been waiting for her whole life.

'What rubbish!' she whispered softly as her practical mind finally took control. She might still daydream about meeting her perfect man some day, but she'd known for a long time that it would never be Nick Howell. Still, there was no harm in indulging in a bit of wishful thinking, because she could magically erase every one of his annoying traits…such as the way he glared at her every time she so much as smiled at a patient, especially the male ones.

No, her imagination might be putting him in a starring role in her dreams but she knew better than to pin any hopes on them coming true. She had now achieved her goal and was a qualified A and E doctor and had a precious daughter to bring up. That was enough occupation for anyone.

The alarm clock suddenly started its annoying bleeping and another day started with Tash uncharacteristically slow to get washed and dressed.

'Sweetheart, your porridge is going to get cold if you don't get a move on,' she chivvied, going back into the bedroom. 'I've put a sprinkle of brown sugar on the…' Her words faded into nothing as she caught sight of the enormous bruise on her daughter's slender arm. Tash seemed completely unconcerned as she slid her arm into the sleeve of her blouse to cover it, almost as if she was indifferent to its existence.

It might be out of sight, but it certainly wasn't out of mind as far as Libby was concerned. For a moment, she was so shocked at the sight that she could barely breathe, let alone find the words to ask what had happened to cause the bruise. Then the possibilities deluged over her and in spite of her training in taking a good case history, she couldn't find the words to ask.

Had there been a simple accident in the playground or the classroom, or was Tash being bullied at school? Was that why she'd been growing more and more subdued since they'd moved? Was that why she'd had that awful nosebleed the other day?

It was hard to believe. The school had seemed to have such a pleasant, happy atmosphere when she'd been shown around that she hadn't even thought to ask about their policy in case of bullying. Anyway, she'd always thought her bouncy friendly daughter was the least likely candidate to be a victim. Had she just been complacent? Should she have been paying more attention? As if she had *time* to be more attentive with the stresses of the new job pulling her in every direction, especially with Nick Howell's all-seeing eyes following her every move.

Which reminded her, she thought with a sudden start, catching sight of the clock and realising that she was going to be late if she didn't get a move on, and of course he would be there with his eyebrow raised to tell her he'd noticed her tardiness.

'Breakfast's ready, Tash,' she said, shelving the idea of asking any questions for the moment. Something that important couldn't be done with one eye on the clock and before she broached the possibility of bullying with her daughter, she wanted to have a word with her teacher—Judy Peverill, was it?—to see if she knew what was going on.

And if she *did*, and if she hadn't done anything about it…

'Don't borrow trouble,' Libby murmured under her breath, waving to Tash as she disappeared inside her friend's front door, knowing that she was safe until she was delivered to school. 'You just need to wait until you can have a word with her teacher. There's no point in getting worked up until you know what's going on... *Rats!* I'll get worked up as much as I like!' she exploded as she struggled to manoeuvre the car into a space that wasn't really big enough for comfort, the memory of Tash's bruised arm all too clear. 'It had better be a one-off event, *and* there had better be a damned good reason why I wasn't informed about what's going on in that school.'

'Libby,' Nick called almost as soon as she set foot inside the department, and a wash of heat suffused her face at the memory of the last time she'd heard him speak her name. Well, she hadn't heard him exactly, and the look in his eyes had been far more romantic than...

'There was a phone call for you,' he said, drawing her to one side of the corridor, but his strangely confidential manner didn't really prepare her for the shock of his next words. 'It was someone from your daughter's school ringing to say she's on her way in.'

'On her way?' Libby repeated stupidly. 'What? Here?' She felt her eyes widen as the shock hit her, her heart leaping into her throat before plunging down to her feet. 'Oh, God…!' Guilt hit her like an avalanche.

What had happened to her precious daughter? It had only been minutes since she'd dropped Tash off at her friend's house. It couldn't possibly be *there* that she was being abused, could it? Oh, why hadn't she asked Tash where she'd got those bruises? She should have, as soon as she'd seen them. She'd never forgive herself if…

'Libby?' Nick took her arm and guided her out of the way of a trolley moving purposefully towards the lifts. She barely glanced at the coterie of staff or at the equipment surrounding the patient obviously in urgent need of surgery. All she could think of was her daughter.

'You've gone as white as a sheet. You're not going to pass out, are you?' he demanded, clearly concerned.

'No, I'm not,' she said firmly, making her way towards the entrance where her daughter would arrive and trying to ignore the feeling that she might be sick. 'Who was it that phoned? What did they say?'

'I didn't speak to them myself. Because you hadn't arrived, the message that she's on her way in came to me.' There was an unaccustomed frown of concern pinching his forehead. 'Is there a problem with your daughter's health?'

'No!' Libby denied in a knee-jerk reaction before adding, uncertainly, 'At least, there never has before, but this morning...' She paused to choose her words, not wanting to cast aspersions on an innocent person, but her overriding concern for Tash came above everything else. 'This morning, I noticed some bruising and... Oh, Nick, I think she's being bullied.'

'What did she say when you asked her?' His frown had grown darker, sharing her reaction to the thought that anyone would mistreat an innocent child.

'I didn't,' she admitted, her guilty feeling growing by the second. 'I was so shocked when I saw the bruising and when I realised that she seemed to be totally unconcerned by it, I didn't know how to ask. Anyway, there's never enough time that early in the morning to sit down and find the right words for a discussion. I was planning to phone the school today, the first time there was a break, and have a word with her teacher. Then I was going to talk to Tash tonight.' She drew in a shuddering breath. 'If anything's happened to her because I didn't...'

'Mummy!' called a muffled voice, and there was Tash, another blood-stained cloth held against her face. 'It did it again,' she wailed as Libby swept her up into her arms and cradled her precious child close.

'What happened, Layla?' Libby demanded of her friend even as she was leading the way to the closest vacant cubicle. 'Were Tash and Mia having an argument?'

'They weren't even in the same room,' Layla Rafik said instantly, putting a consoling arm around her wide-eyed daughter. 'Mia was upstairs, brushing her teeth, and Tash was talking to me in the kitchen while I did the washing-up.'

Libby had never had cause to doubt Layla's word before and didn't need to see her face to know she was telling the truth now. Even so, it took seeing Nick approaching with the appropriate supplies and requesting to take a blood sample from her daughter to get her brain working logically again.

'You think she's anaemic?' she said with a sudden feeling of relief, realising that it was a diagnosis that would explain the series of symptoms Tash had been exhibiting. She was certainly pale enough and lacking in her usual boundless energy. As for the bruising and bleeding, they were such classic signs that she should have realised it herself...she probably would have if it had been any other patient brought into the department.

'There's a reason why it's called a diagnostic test,' Nick said gruffly, handing the labelled sample to a waiting porter with instructions to make sure the lab knew it was a priority. 'In the meantime, it's time to put a large cork in this girl to stop her leaking all over the place,' he teased Tash.

'Do you want me to wait with you?' Layla asked with a quick glance at her watch, and Libby suddenly realised that bringing Tash to the hospital had probably made her friend late for work. 'I did notify the school that I'd be late arriving and that Mia and Tash were with me. We could keep you company while you wait for the results.'

'You and Mia need to get to school, Layla,' she said, sidestepping the question. She would have liked having her support while she waited for the blood tests to be processed but that would just be selfish. 'I'll give you a ring at lunchtime to let you know what's happening.'

'I can always come and pick Tash up after school ends to save you having to miss any more of your shifts,' Layla offered, already sidling towards the door. 'She can curl up on my couch as easily as yours.'

'I'll let you know,' Libby said, even though she knew it wouldn't feel right to let anyone else take care of her sick child for her. Her circumstances might be far from ideal but her mothering instincts had always been strong, right from the first moment she'd known she was pregnant. She would fight to protect her daughter with the last breath in her body.

'See you later, Tash,' Mia called with a wave as she followed her mother out through the curtain. 'I'll tell Mrs Peverill you got another bleeding nose.'

'Perhaps that's something *you* ought to do, Libby,' Nick pointed out softly, his voice reaching her over his shoulder as he gently palpated the glands in Tash's throat. It wasn't until she saw him recording his findings in an admission file that would accompany a patient when they were admitted to a ward that Libby realised he'd been quietly going through the basics of a thorough preliminary examination.

Libby was torn. She knew that it was important for her to notify Tash's teacher what had happened but the last thing she wanted to do was leave her, even with someone she trusted as much as Nick. Anyway, the very fact that he was being so thorough was scaring her. She couldn't bear the thought that he was even contemplating the possibility that there was something more than simple anaemia to worry about.

'Use the phone in here if you'd rather not let her out of your sight,' he suggested kindly, reminding her to 'Press nine to be connected for an outside line,' as though he knew her brain wouldn't be working properly.

Classes had already started so Libby had to be content with asking the school secretary to pass on a message to Judy Peverill that Tash wouldn't be attending school today. Quite what she was going to do with her daughter when she was ready to be released from A and E was another matter because Libby really didn't want to have to miss any more work. She desperately wanted to be with Tash but it just wasn't fair on her colleagues when they were already short-staffed.

Then the test results came back and all her other concerns became academic.

'Sit down, Libby,' Nick advised, and her stomach took a sickening dive when she realised that his face was suddenly devoid of expression.

That was not good. He only looked like that when he had really bad news to tell someone and this couldn't be that bad...could it?

'Of course, we need to do more tests for a definitive diagnosis...a lumbar puncture, a bone-marrow sample,' he began when she shook her head, stupidly feeling as if she needed to be standing on her own two feet when he gave her the news, and gestured for him to continue.

Thoughts were whirling hollowly round inside her head so that she could barely take in what he was saying about the preliminary results and their severity. *Anaemia...abnormal blood cell count...blasts...reticulocytes...platelets...* They were words that she'd studied long and hard to remember, drumming into her head their significance in the workings of the human body, but at this moment they may as well have been in some obscure foreign language.

Only one word made any terrible sense.

'*Leukaemia?*' Libby whispered, collapsing onto the edge of the bed when her knees suddenly refused to bear her weight. She shook her head in stunned disbelief. 'It can't be. Not Tash.'

'Mummy?' Tash whimpered softly, and her eyes were wide with fear, her face paler than ever. 'Does that mean I'm going to die?'

CHAPTER FIVE

AM I going to die?

Tash's words haunted Libby, interrupting her thoughts and bringing a new dimension to her nightmares.

'Of *course* you're not going to die,' she soothed over and over again, even as Tash confided tearfully about a classmate's older sister losing her fight against the disease. 'Treatment has improved since then,' she promised as she accompanied her precious daughter up to the ward, hoping that her explanation sounded more confident than she felt. She was all too conscious, in spite of her concentration, that word was spreading like wildfire through the department. She'd almost been able to feel the pity in the eyes that followed them into the lift on their way to the children's oncology department, and in the midst of her terror, a fierce determination had been born that this was one fight she was not going to lose.

'Hey, squirt, how are you doing?' David ffrench asked as he came towards Tash's bed with a shiny purple balloon in tow.

Libby tried to smile at him but she was too tired to make much of an effort. She couldn't remember when she'd last slept for more than a few minutes at a time.

'I don't like being sick,' Tash said with a tearful wobble to her voice, and Libby's heart squeezed with the agony of knowing there was nothing she could do to make this any easier for her precious baby. The anti-emetics just didn't seem to make any difference to that unfortunate side-effect of the chemotherapy and Tash was miserable.

'I could tell you a story to try to take your mind off it, or I could come back another time,' he offered with a touch of diffidence completely at odds with his professional persona, and Libby could see why Leah was so certain he would make a good father for their child.

Tash grudgingly admitted that she would enjoy having a story read to her and Libby stifled the urge to say something. She'd offered exactly the same diversion only a few minutes ago and had been refused. Still, she could hardly blame the youngster. This first course of chemotherapy was due to last for five days and there were still two more to go, so any respite in the form of someone willing to entertain Tash would at least give her a few minutes to close her eyes.

'You look exhausted,' David murmured, and she forced herself to open her eyes. Immediately, her gaze flew across to the bed.

'She's asleep,' he reassured her with a gentle smile, and she was struck anew by the familiarity of those blue-green eyes. Anyone who didn't know better might almost think he was Tash's father. 'I'm sorry she's having a hard time of it.

There's really no rhyme or reason why one patient reacts so much more severely than another.'

'I know. And the sickness and diarrhoea seem to be getting worse by the hour.' Libby sighed. 'At least her blood count hasn't started dropping yet, or her hair falling out.'

'Such pretty hair, just like her mother's,' he complimented easily. 'At least you know better than most parents that it'll grow back once the chemo's finished.'

'Not that it'll be much consolation to an eight-year-old,' she said wryly. 'They can't bear waiting a week for Christmas so waiting months for their hair to grow will seem like for ever.' One part of her brain was marvelling that she was having such a mundane conversation with the man. When she'd first come to work at St Luke's she'd barely been able to force herself to look in his direction, but since he'd been dropping in to Tash's room at odd times over the last three days, it was beginning to feel almost as if she'd known him all her life.

The thought was a warming one and lasted

until he had to silence his pager and hurry back to the department to monitor a suspected placental abruption in one of his IVF mothers.

Unfortunately, once he left Tash's room, the loneliness of her existence descended again. Now that her mother was gone, there was nobody in her life to share the burden of waiting to see how well Tash's body responded to the treatment; nobody to talk to in the black moments when exhaustion made her fear the worst; nobody to wrap her in a comforting hug and tell her reassuring things.

'You look like something the cat dragged in,' Nick growled into the darkness behind her eyelids and she didn't know whether to laugh or burst into tears.

'Thank you for those few kind words,' she said quietly, marvelling that her heart had summoned the energy to pump so fast just at the sound of his voice.

'I bet you haven't even been home since she was admitted,' he continued, ignoring her attempt at irony, or was it sarcasm? She was really too tired to care.

'You'd lose the bet,' she said, feeling so guilty that she had to force herself to meet his critical gaze because she knew that he was basically right. The only time she'd gone home in the last three dreadful days had been to collect clothing and toiletries for Tash and herself. Other than that, every minute had been spent at the hospital, either working her scheduled shifts or at Tash's bedside.

He raised a sceptical eyebrow and muttered something under his breath.

'Well, while she's asleep, you can come with me for a few minutes,' he said, putting a hand under her elbow to urge her to her feet.

If she hadn't been half-asleep she would have been quicker to ask what he thought he was doing. After all, she'd finished her shift several hours ago. As it was, by the time her brain had caught up with her feet, he was leading her into the little staff kitchen just round the corner from Tash's room.

'Sit yourself down,' he ordered, turning to the humming microwave just as the bell sounded. 'You look as if you haven't eaten in a week,' he said as he turned with a steaming plate and set it in front of her.

His unexpected kindness was the final straw.

'I can't eat anything,' she said dully. 'I haven't got any appetite.'

'That's because you're too tired and too wound up,' he said grimly, adding a small bowl of salad and a tall glass of orange juice to the spread. 'David ffrench told me you've been spending every spare minute up here—that you haven't left your daughter's side when you aren't on duty—but I didn't need him to tell me you're on the point of collapse.'

'David ffrench told you…?' she wasn't certain whether to be angry with the man for interfering or moved that he'd cared enough to comment.

'He's concerned about you. We all are,' he added, almost fiercely, as if the words couldn't be held back. 'I can't imagine how you must be feeling.'

She was touched.

Until that moment, she'd been feeling numb and so…so *alone*.

'It certainly feels different from the other side,' she said. 'I was arrogant enough to think that my training meant I would be able to cope better with all this but…' She shook her head. 'I think it's worse.'

'Because you know too much,' he agreed. 'You know all the things that can go wrong and, of course, you spend all your time watching every little thing because you're convincing yourself that they *are* going wrong.'

'That sounds like the voice of experience. Was it a family member?' She swiftly banished the thought that Nick might have lost a child, as well as the sudden free-fall feeling inside her at the thought that there had been someone that special in his life. It was none of her business who he was close to, just that it would never be her.

'My father,' he said, and she saw the fleeting shadow of concern in his eyes. 'He had a major heart attack…wouldn't have survived at all if he hadn't been in the hospital to undergo some tests when it happened.'

'How is he now?' She hated to ask, superstitious that Tash's recovery in some way depended on his father's survival.

'He's in Russia,' Nick said with a grin.

'Russia!' It was the last answer she'd expected.

'It was the first thing my mother said to him when he regained consciousness—that he wasn't allowed to die because he'd promised to take her to Russia to visit all her relatives there.'

'And he recovered well enough to go, even after the heart attack? That's a long flight, isn't it?'

'He had to have a quadruple bypass first, but he's in better health than he's been for years,' Nick said, then added with a grin, 'He doesn't have any option with my mother supervising his tablets, watching every bite he eats and going walking with him to make sure he takes enough exercise. She says it's taken her forty years to get him trained and she doesn't want to have to break in a new husband so she's taking great care of the one she's got!'

Libby joined in his laughter as a vague memory suddenly became clearer. 'She's Russian, isn't she?' Another thought surfaced and she spoke before she had time to monitor her words. 'And you're not Nicholas. You're Nikolai. And that's why she calls you...Kolya.'

The strange mixture of expressions that crossed his face then made her wish she'd kept her mouth shut, especially when he looked so forbidding. But how did she apologise when she didn't know what she'd said to put that look there? It couldn't be that she'd mentioned his Russian ancestry— she knew it wasn't a secret because he'd told her that his parents were visiting his mother's relatives there, just a few minutes ago.

She dropped her eyes away from the piercing accusation in his and discovered that she'd almost cleared the plate he'd given her without realising that she'd been eating. Suddenly, her appetite fled and she pushed the plate away.

'Thank you for that, but if I eat any more I'll be the size of a house,' she excused herself, falling back on well-practised lines from the days when she'd had such difficulty managing her weight.

'I've seen more fat on a cold chip!' Nick scowled impatiently. 'You're going to need your strength if you're going to be any use to your daughter.' He clamped his lips shut as though briefly regretting making a personal comment, then continued decisively. 'In fact, I think it would be a good idea if you took some time off to be with her. Trying to do a full shift as well as keeping her company is just going to exhaust you, and it won't be doing your concentration much good either.'

'In an ideal world, that's exactly what I'd do,' Libby agreed stiffly, resenting his easy assumption that he knew what was best. 'But in the absence of a win on the lottery and with bills to pay, I'll be working as usual.' She bit her lip when she realised how ungrateful she sounded, especially when he'd been so thoughtful as to bring her a meal.

He glowered at her and for a moment she thought he was going to retaliate with a noisy broadside. Instead, he retreated behind an expressionless mask and warned her softly. 'You'll only continue working as usual until I consider you're so tired that you're putting the patients at risk…and that won't be very long if you don't get some sleep.'

His feet were almost silent as he strode out of the room, leaving her feeling sick.

'He's right, of course,' she whispered miserably, knowing that familiar feeling of being trapped between a rock and a hard place. She needed to be with Tash every bit as much as her daughter needed her to be there; she couldn't expect a little girl to go through such treatment alone without losing her sanity.

But she also needed to earn a living. She certainly couldn't afford to lose her job at St Luke's, not if she was ever going to be able to afford a nicer house for the two of them.

She felt the hot press of tears behind her eyes and fought them back, refusing to give in to the futile anger that she was having to cope with everything alone. If her mother hadn't died…

'Enough!' She blinked her eyes furiously and drew in a steadying breath, straightening her shoulders with renewed determination for the task ahead. 'If she hadn't died, I wouldn't have found out that we're *not* alone in the world. And it just became more important than ever to find out about that family.'

For just a second she let herself contemplate the worst-case scenario—that Tash didn't respond to the chemotherapy and needed to find a bone-marrow donor to save her life—and realised that she couldn't afford to put it off much longer if she needed time to persuade people to be tested for compatibility.

She closed her eyes, dreading the fallout from the chaos she was going to bring into innocent lives that didn't deserve it. Then she heard Tash whimper and retch weakly and even as she hurried to her side to position the disposable basin, she knew that she would do anything for her precious child. Anything.

'Leah?' she said hesitantly into the phone several hours later when Tash was once again sleeping. 'This is Libby Cornish... I don't know if you remember me?'

'Of course I remember you,' the voice on the other end said warmly, and Libby allowed herself to relax briefly, glad that it hadn't been David who'd answered. 'What can I do for you?'

Suddenly, her carefully worded, painfully rehearsed explanation disappeared and she couldn't remember anything but the reason why she'd needed to make contact.

'I don't know if your husband told you, but, my daughter, Tash...Natasha...is having chemotherapy for leukaemia,' she blurted, her thoughts so fragmented that she couldn't marshal them into any sort of logical order. 'David came to visit her today, on the ward. He cheered her up for a while but...I was thinking...in case it doesn't work and Tash doesn't go into remission, she would need...' She couldn't go on, every word sticking in her throat with the enormity of what she was doing.

Although the silence from the other end of the line only lasted seconds, it seemed to go on for ever before she heard a soft expression of comprehension.

'Where are you?' Leah demanded briskly. 'At the hospital?'

'The chemo's making Tash very sick and miserable so I'm spending as much time as I can with her, between my shifts in A and E,' Libby explained.

Within a couple of minutes Leah had efficiently determined Libby's movements for the next couple of days before she grew silent for a moment.

'Libby…' She paused for the first time since she'd gone into organisation mode and Libby wondered uneasily what was coming next. She should have guessed that David's wife wouldn't beat about the bush. 'I was just wondering why it had taken you so long to make contact, but it's really none of my business,' she admitted cheerfully. 'I'm just glad that you're finally doing it, even if it's something so awful that's pushed you into it. Just leave everything to me and I'll be in contact soon.'

Libby put the phone down feeling as if she'd just had a close encounter with a small tornado, but she couldn't help smiling. It had been several months since she'd first been introduced to the woman David had married but she'd never forget that it had only taken a few seconds before her keen eyes had been flicking between David and Libby. It spoke volumes for the woman's self-control that she'd never voiced a single one of the questions Libby had seen in her eyes.

Well, Libby thought with an uncomfortable mixture of dread and anticipation, it wouldn't be long now before Leah had all the answers. In the meantime…

'Oh, hell, I'm going to be late if I don't run,' she muttered when she caught sight of the time.

She paused briefly beside Tash's bed, her heart aching that her bright, bubbly daughter should lie there looking so pale and wan. If she could take her place…

Futile thought, she knew as she stroked a gentle hand over that dark hair that made her look so much paler and mourned the fact that it would soon be falling out in handfuls. She bent down to feather a kiss at her temple. 'I love you, sweetheart,' she whispered, not wanting to wake her from her sleep, knowing she needed the time to gather her strength between the debilitating bouts of nausea. 'I'll be back soon.'

'Oh, my God!' somebody shrieked within seconds of Libby reporting for the start of her shift, the sound high-pitched and horrified.

For an instant the usual hubbub of the department was silenced, only to be replaced by a chorus of shouts and screams.

Libby's feet were moving before she realised it, the direction of the patients' gazes guiding her to the cause of the problem.

'She's had her throat cut!' someone cried.

'She's dead!' exclaimed another.

'*Do* something!' several were shouting, even as Libby caught her first sight of the victim.

She was so young, was her first thought as she dropped to her knees beside the slight body on the floor. *There's so much blood...too much,* was her second as she reached out gloved hands towards the crimson-sodden fabric pressed against the olive-toned skin of the woman's neck.

Then dark eyes opened and stared up at her,

dazed and terrified, and she was shocked to realise that the young girl was still alive.

'Hello. My name's Libby. I'm a doctor,' she began as she usually did, then, as the slender fingers fell away, their strength clearly exhausted, she realised the severity of the problem. 'I need some help here, fast!' she shouted as she took over the girl's trembling attempts to stem the blood pouring out of the obscene gash. As though he'd answered her silent prayer, Nick appeared at her side.

'What have we got?' he demanded, even as his gloved hands began their own rapid examination, both of them oblivious to their horrified audience.

'As far as I can tell, the carotid's been completely severed, but I daren't take the pressure off to look too closely. She's already lost far too much blood. Her pulse is weak and thready and she's about to go into shock.'

Even as she was speaking, more staff arrived to help lift the young woman onto a trolley to take her through to the nearest resuscitation room, the whole process made much more difficult because Libby didn't dare to move her hands.

In spite of her best efforts, blood was still spurting out between her fingers and the IVs that were being inserted in every available vein were going to have to be run wide open if they were going to make an appreciable difference.

Meanwhile, Nick was snapping out commands, calling for an immediate consult from a vascular surgeon then countermanding himself to order a theatre to be made ready even as he sent a blood sample off at a run for urgent cross-matching.

Libby didn't even look up to see what was happening around them. Her whole concentration was divided between maintaining pressure on the gaping wound under her fingers and the dark pleading eyes that never left her face even as she murmured a litany of encouraging words.

It was the appearance of the first silent tear, sliding between thick dark lashes and into the wealth of lustrous dark hair at her temple, that nearly broke Libby's heart.

'Sweetheart, we're doing everything we can,'

she promised, knowing that Nick was already preparing to isolate and clamp the severed artery to prevent any further blood loss. 'Can you tell me your name?'

The young woman, barely more than a girl, really, now that she could see her more closely, frowned as though struggling for comprehension. Suddenly, Libby realised that they might have another problem.

'I think we need some kind of interpreter,' she warned, and heard someone groan at the added complication. 'Well, it might just be the shock of what's happened to her, but I'm not sure she understands what we're saying to her.'

'Preferably a female interpreter,' Nick tacked on as the request went out, then added in an aside. 'I might be wrong, but this has the hallmarks of what the press insists on calling an "honour" killing.'

'How can anyone call *this* honourable?' Libby demanded, her heart going out to the traumatised young woman even more at the thought that her own family could have done this to her. 'It's nothing more than a blatant attempt at murder.'

'And that's exactly how the police will treat it,' Nick promised grimly as he waited for the anaesthetic to take effect before he could start work. 'They've had years of abuse from ethnic minorities complaining that the authorities don't respect their traditions, but there's a world of difference between arranged marriages and a forced marriage.'

'I think you ought to stop scowling,' Libby suggested softly, a reassuring smile on her face for their patient and the translator who had just hurried in to join them. 'You're scaring every-one within a thirty-yard radius.'

'Sorry,' he murmured as he bent towards the young woman. When she flinched away from him, Libby saw his hands clench in anger at the man who had instilled such fear in her. 'Can you tell her that I'm going to help her?' he said quietly to the translator, pointing to her neck then miming the act of sewing. 'Tell her you'll be here to ex-plain everything as soon as it's all finished. OK?'

Obviously, he had finished with the one word that she had no difficulty understanding even without a translator, but even though the words were now comprehensible, still she looked towards Libby with a question in her eyes.

Libby smiled and nodded reassuringly, hoping she seemed relaxed in spite of the fact that her fingers were beginning to cramp badly from being forced to maintain their position for so long. 'OK,' she encouraged.

'OK,' the young woman mouthed, any sound she made so soft that it was completely lost in the clatter of the activity going on around her. Then, with one last pleading look from Libby to Nick, she closed her eyes in a gesture of trust.

'Right, everybody, we've only got one chance to get this right and only one way to do it...fast and accurate,' Nick said softly when the translator stepped back out of the way, and Libby realised that he was deliberately keeping his tone conversational because that would be the least likely to frighten their patient. 'We've managed to get some fluids into her and brought her blood pressure up from the floor, but as soon as Libby takes the pressure off that carotid…'

He didn't need to finish the sentence. They all knew just how quickly a patient could exsanguinate from such a catastrophic wound to one of the major blood vessels in the body. The only way they were going to prevent that happening was if Nick managed to isolate the damaged ends as quickly as possible and get some clamps on them. The problem was, he was going to be working blind, unable to see what he was looking for in an area awash with the blood that would be pumped out of the patient's body at high pressure with every terrified beat of her heart.

Afterwards, Libby couldn't have said how long the procedure had taken, but she was convinced that she'd held her breath throughout. The room quickly looked like a slaughterhouse as the bright blood sprayed and dripped while Nick probed the vulnerable neck for the ends of the damaged vessel. Under his breath Libby could hear a constant litany of incomprehensible words. She guessed he was speaking

Russian, but whether he was reciting prayers or every swear word he knew she had no idea.

'Squeeze that blood in faster,' he growled, without taking his eyes off his task, his voice harsh with strain as the monitors began to shrill and bleep their warnings of impending disaster. In spite of all their efforts and the number of IVs attempting to replace the catastrophic loss, the woman's blood volume was still dropping faster than it could be replaced when, almost as if a tap had been turned off, Nick's exclamation of success told them that he'd managed to position the vital clamp.

They were all holding their breath, waiting to see whether it was holding, when the door swung open to admit a harried-looking man, his hair standing on end as if he'd either just run his fingers through it, or had pulled off a surgical cap.

'Good God!' he exclaimed when he caught sight of the bloody chaos surrounding them, then his eyes homed in on the monitors charting the fact that their patient was actually beginning to stabilise now that she wasn't bleeding any more.

'Hi, Felix. I'm glad it's you,' Nick welcomed him.

'Tell me,' the hospital's senior vascular surgeon demanded succinctly, holding a mask over his face as he leant towards the brightly illuminated neck.

'Carotid, obviously,' Nick said, equally succinctly. 'It's been completely severed. Sharp instrument used, so it shouldn't be too difficult for you to darn it back together. I haven't had a chance to check for any other damaged structures in her neck but her trachea is apparently undamaged and she still has full use of all her extremities. You might want to get Plastics to tidy up after you... Oh, and there are a couple of defensive wounds on her arms that will need attention, too.'

'Have you got any more blood ordered or have you used it all for decorating in here?'

'It's being cross-matched as we speak.' Libby watched Nick as he stripped his gloves off and aimed them into the bin, the whole process purely automatic as he didn't once take his eyes off the preparations being made to transfer their barely stable patient up to Theatre.

'Right, then, I'll leave it to you to get her upstairs safely. I'll go up and start scrubbing,' Felix said as he strode briskly towards the door. At the last possible moment he said, 'By the way, that was a good save, Nick. You've got a good team down here,' throwing the words nonchalantly over his shoulder before he disappeared.

Libby saw the grin of appreciation on Nick's face, in spite of the speed they were working at to get their patient transported to Theatre as quickly as possible. She could feel a similar one on her own face, pleased that their skills had been recognised. All she could do now was keep her fingers crossed that they'd done enough, soon enough, not only to save their patient's life but to do it before she'd suffered any permanent damage to her brain or other essential organs.

'Please. I am Nusin Dolen,' said a young woman just as Libby was about to finish her shift and go back up to Tash.

Libby frowned, unable to place the name, although from the way the young woman was smiling at her, she seemed to expect Libby to recognise her.

'I'm sorry, Ms Dolen…?'

She laughed. 'Call me Nusin, and it is my fault for not explaining properly. If you remember, I am the interpreter who was called to help Halima Siddiqui today.'

'Halima Siddiqui?' Libby still wasn't any wiser.

'The girl who had her throat cut,' Nusin added softly as several people passed close by. She was clearly concerned for their patient's confidentiality.

'Oh! I didn't know her name!' Libby exclaimed. 'How is she? I was going to phone to find out how her operation went.'

'She asked me to come and find you. She would like you to come up to see her so that she can thank you for saving her life.'

'Oh, but I was only one of the team,' Libby demurred, uncomfortable at being singled out. 'It was Nick…Dr Howell…who stopped the bleeding, and Felix, the vascular surgeon, who made the repair.'

'But she said that you were the one who held her life in your hands,' Nusin insisted softly. 'She told me that you were the one who put your hands on her throat to stop the blood coming out, and that you were looking at her as if you were willing her to stay alive. That was how I knew she was talking about you,' she added when Libby would have demurred again. 'She described your eyes…that unusual colour halfway between blue and green, calm and deep like the sea.'

Now Libby was blushing and, purely to end the embarrassing conversation, agreed to pay a quick visit as soon as she had changed her clothes.

Ten minutes later she was directed to a curtained cubicle by the ward sister.

'The interpreter is already in with her,' she said with a smile. 'Perhaps you can persuade her to tell you what happened to her. The police couldn't get her to say anything.'

Libby was uncomfortable with the idea that

she might be asked to browbeat Halima in any way, but she *had* promised to visit her.

'You are here!' Halima exclaimed in a hoarse voice as soon as she saw Libby standing at the gap in the curtains, her dark eyes shining with sudden tears as she beckoned her closer. 'Come! Please, come!'

There was still an IV line snaking into the back of one hand and the dressings covering the wounds at her throat and arms were stark white against the silky olive of her skin.

Propped weakly against the pile of pillows, she seemed even younger than she had when she'd collapsed on the floor of the A and E department, little more than a child, and Libby found it more difficult than ever to understand why anyone would try to murder her.

'How are you feeling?' She glanced across at the interpreter, expecting her to start speaking, but before Nusin could say a word, Halima was replying.

'Alive and very grateful to you,' she said huskily, 'but very frightened, too.'

'But…you don't need an interpreter?' Libby was startled. She'd expected to have one of those slightly frustrating conversations that took twice as long to get a simple answer, but other than a slightly strained quality to her voice that could easily be put down to the result of the anaesthetic tube during her recent surgery, it seemed that Halima was perfectly able to answer for herself.

'I have been studying your language for a year, ever since I knew I was going to university.'

'University?' She barely looked old enough for secondary school.

'If I could tell you, to spare Halima's voice?' Nusin offered, and went on to explain that in her own country Halima had been discovered to be nothing short of a mathematical genius when she had been very young and that her father had been determined that, in the absence of a son, his eldest daughter would one day be the source of the family's fortune.

'In the nearest city he was told about an internet site where people look for wives and husbands of their own…ethnicity?' Libby nodded. She'd heard something about that a while ago. In fact, someone at her last hospital had gone on several dates with people she'd found that way, but they'd all been similar professional people in their late twenties and thirties, certainly not children.

'It wasn't until Halima arrived here and was introduced to Renan, a man in his late thirties, that she discovered that her father had promised her in marriage in return for her university expenses being paid and the rest of her family being set up in this country.' Nusin was trying hard, for Halima's sake, to keep the condemnation out of her voice but Libby could still hear her opinion of a father who would do such a thing.

'She is not yet sixteen,' Nusin went on, 'and she has no wish to marry before going to university, and when she told her father that she refused to marry this man as old as her father…'

'He said I had dishonoured the family,' Halima said brokenly, tears now pouring down her cheeks. 'He said that the family could never go back home because I had shamed them, and if I refused to marry Renan, they would have nowhere to live here and no money to pay him back for our travel.'

'This is why Halima does not wish to speak to the police,' Nusin explained before Libby had a chance to ask. 'She does not want anyone to know that she is alive because they will try again to kill her.'

Before she left Halima's bedside, Libby promised, reluctantly, to keep their secret a little longer, but she hadn't promised not to try to find a solution.

Her brain was busily trying to work out the best way of wording hypothetical questions to educational and legal establishments to find out if there was any way of unravelling the situation when her pager went off, and the only thought left in her head was Tash.

CHAPTER SIX

'LIBBY, this is Leah. Leah ffrench,' said the voice on the other end when she reached the nearest phone with her heart in her mouth.

'Leah?' Her legs were so weak they were barely able to support her. As she was no longer on duty she'd been utterly convinced that the call must be about her daughter.

'I didn't know whether you were still finishing your shift in A and E...knowing that you can't always clock off on time if you're in the middle of a case...or whether you were on your way to your daughter.'

'I was just visiting one of the patients we admitted earlier today,' Libby said weakly, her heart still beating at twice the speed of light. 'Then I was going up to Tash…in fact, I thought something had happened to Tash when you paged me.'

'Oh, Libby! I'm *so* sorry! I just didn't think! That would be your obvious reaction,' Leah apologised profusely, then asked, 'Listen, can you meet us in the relatives' room at the other end of Tash's floor in half an hour?'

'Us?' Libby's brain was still worrying about a sudden worsening of Tash's health and couldn't work out why Leah would be included in a conference with the oncology team treating her daughter.

'I'll have David and Maggie with me,' Leah said, and suddenly Libby's focus switched in the right direction. After months of vacillation and worry she had reached the point of no return and she didn't really have an option, not with Tash's health at risk.

She just had one question for Leah.

'How did you guess?' she demanded. 'How did you put everything together? I was certain I'd covered my tracks so that I wouldn't cause problems for…for your family.'

'Actually, it was simple,' Leah said, her warm chuckle reaching Libby down the phone line to soothe some of the tension for a moment. 'It was the unusual colour of your eyes…unless I've got the whole situation completely wrong? No, don't tell me now. Wait till we're all together to give me the details. In half an hour?'

Libby agreed with more than a hint of trepidation, suddenly wondering if she was making an enormous mistake.

Her thoughts were in turmoil as she tried to persuade Tash to eat something, her own stomach rebelling at the mere sight of food because she was so tense. Then, just as she was trying to find an excuse to leave her daughter for her meeting, Nick appeared in the doorway and scattered what little wits she had left.

'Hey, princess, are you any good at computers?'

'What sort of computers?' Tash responded listlessly, her eyes only brightening as he took a slim top-of-the-range laptop out from behind his back. Libby only knew that it was far and away more sophisticated than the one her daughter had been coveting, hoping for an extra-special birthday present.

'The sort of computer that's stuffed with hundreds of games,' he said enticingly, nudging Libby aside with a seemingly casual bump of his hip as he set the thing up on Tash's table and switched it on. 'If we send your mum off to get something to eat, we could see if there's anything interesting on here... But I hope you're good at this, because I really don't like beating people too easily.'

'*No* chance!' Tash said fervently. 'I'm already the best in my class at school. I've got the highest scores on *everything*.'

Libby watched, bemused, as Nick quickly had Tash helping him to connect up the game controls, her nausea apparently banished temporarily by the novelty and the prospect of battle.

'Are you still here?' he demanded a moment later with a glance in Libby's direction and a smile of complicity for Tash. 'There's no point standing there, hoping you're going to be invited to play. Not this time. This is just between the princess and me and it's going to be a fight to the death!'

'That's right, Mum. To the death!' Tash agreed with relish. 'You go and get something to eat. You can come back when I've had time to beat Dr…'

'Nick,' he supplied before Libby had a chance to say anything.

'Dr Nick,' Tash said approvingly, her eyes already beginning to glow with the gleam of battle that Libby hadn't seen for far too long.

Nick's eyes met hers above Tash's bent head and when he raised a questioning eyebrow and pointedly glanced down at his watch she suddenly realised that she was still standing there watching the two of them together, marvelling at the instant rapport they seemed to have struck up.

'Thank you,' she mouthed, wondering how he had known that she'd agreed to meet up with Leah and co. five minutes ago.

She knew from working with him that he had an amazing way with their young patients, she mused on her way to the relatives' room, but she hadn't expected Tash to take to Nick so easily, especially when she wasn't feeling well. With no father figure in her life, she'd never had much practice relating to adult males and on the rare occasion when she was ill, she usually preferred to have her mother around to...

Her meandering thoughts ground to a halt when she saw the group of people waiting for her, suddenly wishing she could turn tail and run.

There seemed to be so many of them, too, and every one of them had turned to face her as she appeared in the doorway.

There was Jake Lascelles and his wife Maggie, soon to return to part-time A and E work after the birth of her first child, then there was Maggie's brother David ffrench, the obs and gynae consultant in charge of the hospital's ground-breaking assisted reproduction unit, and his wife Leah who was still on maternity leave from her post in the same department. The only people missing were David and Maggie's parents and the two newest members of the expanding ffrench family.

'Come in, Libby,' Leah invited cheerfully. 'I brought some decent coffee in with me and some calorie nightmares to nibble. Come and make yourself comfortable and grab something before these men hog the lot.'

As an icebreaker, the invitation was perfect, but it was only putting off the evil moment when she would have to tell them...

'So,' Jake said, taking the bull by the horns before she'd even sat down, 'I've got no idea what all this is about, but I'm presuming that it has something to do with the fact that your daughter's undergoing her first round of chemo for leukaemia.'

'Jake! Behave!' Maggie scolded, holding out a loaded plate towards him in a silent instruction to use his mouth for something other than interrogation.

'Let Libby tell us in her own way,' Leah added with a supportive smile in Libby's direction.

'Well, indirectly, he's right,' she began shakily, subsiding onto the edge of the nearest seat. 'As you probably know from the hospital grapevine, Tash was recently diagnosed and is currently on her first round of chemo and going through the miseries of nausea, and so on, but…' She closed her eyes and shook her head, suddenly lost for words. 'Oh, this is so much harder than I thought it would be,' she muttered under her breath as she rose to her feet again, wishing she was anywhere than here with these people…until she remembered that Tash was depending on her and she didn't have an option.

'Would you like me to start the ball rolling?' Leah offered. 'If I start to stray you can set me straight.'

Libby was startled by the suggestion but she could remember the knowing expression on Leah's face from the first time she'd been introduced to her and didn't doubt for a moment that she'd probably managed to put two and two together and come very near the right answer.

But kind though the offer was, it was her story to tell and her responsibility to tell it and nothing would be gained by delaying any longer.

'My mother died just over a year ago...of cancer,' she added as an aside. 'And it wasn't until almost the end—when she was told that the treatment had failed and she realised that Tash and I were going to be all alone in the world—that she finally told me about my father.' She couldn't stay sitting any longer.

She'd hoped that once she'd started talking her voice would grow steadier but instead, the closer she came to the crux of the story she was telling, she realised that it was quivering more than ever. If she hadn't braced herself against the edge of the window-sill she probably wouldn't even have been able to stay on her feet.

'She told me that for years she'd worked for a man who was good and kind and loving but whose marriage was unravelling because his wife had become totally besotted with their newborn son from the moment he was born. She—my mum—had fallen in love with her boss soon after she'd started working with him and, well...' She couldn't go into detail, not about her mother, leaving them to draw their own conclusions about where the relationship had gone during that unhappy time.

'She tried to fool herself that he might leave his wife for her, but when she saw how distraught he was to have broken his vows with her, she realised she was only kidding herself. He loved his wife in spite of the way she had pushed him away in favour of their son.'

The room was so silent that it hardly seemed as if anyone was breathing but she didn't dare look at any of them to check. She didn't think she would be able to continue if she saw condemnation in their eyes when they heard what she had to say next.

'Then she discovered that she was pregnant,' she said baldly, unsurprised to hear a murmur and at least one sharp intake of breath. 'And even though she desperately wanted to be near him, she knew that she couldn't stay if she was going to keep the baby.'

'She could have…' one of the men started, then halted with a grunt. Libby guessed that he'd been silenced by the business end of an elbow but didn't bother to look up to find out. Now that she'd started…

'She didn't even consider an abortion because she couldn't bear to destroy the only part of him she would ever have,' she continued, refusing to remember how different her own decision had been and how much harder. 'So she changed her name to Cornish—the closest she could get to France and the ffrench, she always told me, although I didn't understand the irony of the joke till after she died—and she moved away to bring me up on her own.'

Finally, she knew it was time to face the consequences, but it was so hard to lift her head up to meet the two pairs of eyes that were so uncannily like her own.

'His name isn't on my birth certificate because she couldn't ask his permission to register the fact without telling him of my existence, but…'

'But, even though your name isn't ffrench, you're our sister,' Maggie finished for her, her expression a mixture of shock and delight.

'My God, look at your eyes. They're exactly the same as ours, David. How did we not see it before?'

'You'd be willing to undergo a DNA test to prove it,' her brother challenged, his expression altogether grimmer.

'If you wanted me to, yes,' Libby said firmly, her chin coming up another inch to meet his glare with one of her own. 'But there really isn't any need because I haven't come to try to take anything away from you. I'm far too old to need any financial support; I've been supporting myself ever since I left school.'

'So, why *have* you tracked us down, after all these years?' he demanded. 'Was it just for the satisfaction of rubbing our noses in our father's infidelity?'

'Not at all,' she objected heatedly. 'That was the *last* thing I wanted.'

'So?'

'So, she's already told us why, David,' Maggie said firmly, a growing smile on her face. 'When her mother was dying, she realised that Libby and her daughter would be all alone in the world if she didn't find us…the rest of her family.'

With Maggie's acceptance, Libby was just beginning to let herself think that she'd been worrying for nothing when David returned to the attack.

'Why *now*?' he challenged anew. 'You admitted that you've known about us for more than a year and you've been working at St Luke's for months. Why didn't you say something when you first found us?'

'Initially, I was only looking for you for my own satisfaction,' she said shakily, his apparent anger making her wonder if she'd done the right thing after all. 'I wanted to find you, wanted a chance to meet you casually. I thought there would be plenty of time to work up to telling my daughter that we weren't completely alone in the world. Years, I thought. I certainly didn't want to cause your family any trouble so I had no intention of mentioning our…relationship.'

'So, tell us…what changed your mind?' Leah's question didn't have the sharp edge of David's but, then, she was only a ffrench by marriage.

'I would have thought that was obvious,' Libby said sadly, her heart aching with the weight of her decision. 'When Tash was diagnosed with leukaemia I realised that there was no guarantee how much time she had and that it was important to let her know that she *has* other family...uncles and aunts and cousins. I was hoping that you would be willing to let her get to know you, sooner rather than later. In case...'

She paused just long enough to snatch a shaky breath, refusing to let herself say the words aloud. She was only going to think positive thoughts about Tash's treatment. But, even then, she wasn't foolish enough not to prepare for every eventuality and she steeled herself for the most important part of this whole conversation.

'I was also hoping that, if it became necessary, some of you might be willing to be tested to see if you were compatible as bone-marrow donors.'

There was a pause of several seconds while the stark words seemed to echo around the room—just long enough for Libby's heart to start sinking.

'Of course I'll be tested!' Maggie exclaimed,

as though any other answer was unthinkable, and it was like having the sun come out in the middle of a cloudy day.

David frowned at her. 'Even if you are a match, I doubt you'd be able to be a donor immediately, Maggot. You're still feeding Megan. But there's no reason why *I* couldn't.'

'Well, Tash—I presume that's short for Natasha, is it? I love that name. It was one of the ones I contemplated when I was pregnant,' Maggie said in a smiling aside. 'Anyway, she's only in her first cycle of chemo, and she might never need a donor, but by the time that happened it would be months or even years down the line and I won't be lactating any more.'

Libby was so overwhelmed with relief at their immediate generosity that she didn't know whether to laugh or cry.

'I wasn't sure whether you'd be so angry that I'd tracked you down that you'd refuse to even consider it,' she admitted shakily, sinking down onto the uncomfortable wooden arm of a nearby chair when her knees refused to hold her up any longer.

'Why should we be angry with you? It all happened years ago and it's hardly your fault,' David said without a trace of a frown. 'In fact, the events that led to your existence probably explain some of the things that Maggie and I have never understood about our parents and the dynamics of their marriage.'

Libby didn't pretend to know what they were talking about. She was more interested in her own immediate concerns.

'You'll never know how grateful I am that you're willing to be tested, but... What about Tash? Are you comfortable for her to know that we're related? Would you be willing to let her get to know you or would it be too much of an embarrassment—like airing dirty linen in public? Perhaps we could say we're long-lost cousins, or something?'

'I suppose it could be a problem for our parents,' David admitted with a renewed note of caution. 'They've got a lot of friends and business colleagues in the area.'

'Perhaps you should hold off making any decisions about that until you've spoken to them,' Leah suggested calmly. 'They've only just gone back to New Zealand after playing the doting grandparents—'

'And that's a wonder in itself,' Maggie broke in with a pointed glance in David's direction. 'It must be the first time in his life that Dad's ever won a battle with Mum. She was so determined she was going to move back to England straight away to spend all her spare time with the grandchildren that she was willing to abandon their new home over there with everything in it!'

'But all that doesn't really matter. It doesn't mean that we can't meet Tash and let her get to know us,' David said firmly. 'Apart from our family relationship, we're also colleagues at St Luke's. There's no reason why we can't just visit her to entertain her and keep her spirits up. Then, by the time we've made a decision about any revelations, she'll have got to know us a bit and it won't come as such a shock.'

'Are you sure?' Libby asked, hardly daring to believe that it was going to be this easy.

'Of course we're sure,' Maggie said firmly, then grinned. 'Hey! I've always wanted a sister and now I've got two—you and Leah. And our children are going to have another cousin.'

'And I've just had a great idea, Maggie,' Leah said to her sister-in-law, then turned to Libby with a teasing smile. 'How old is Tash? How long will it be before we can ask her to babysit for us?'

'Opportunist!' David accused even as he joined in the laughter while Libby's heart floated. If *that* hadn't been a sign of acceptance…

'So, when do you want to do it?' Maggie asked, serious once more.

'That depends what "it" you're talking about,' Libby said cautiously. 'If you mean testing for compatibility—'

'That's a given,' she interrupted with a glance at David for his nod of confirmation. 'We'll both be tested as soon as we can so we'll know whether to be prepared to donate if necessary. But I actually meant when do you want to introduce us to Tash? How well is she tolerating the chemo? Is she well enough for visitors?'

'She was looking pretty grim when I saw her,' David said, causing several sets of raised eyebrows. 'That was yesterday, before I knew any of this,' he explained. 'I was visiting one of my IVF mothers—she's a cancer patient, too, and as her treatment will make her sterile, she's stored some fertilised eggs ready to try for a family when she's well again. I caught sight of Tash looking a bit miserable on my way through the department and it wasn't till I stopped for a chat that I discovered she's Libby's daughter.' He turned to Libby. 'She's a lovely child, a real credit to you.'

'Thank you.' Her heart swelled with pride. 'Not that she's feeling very lovely at the moment, and she's really dreading having her hair fall out. She wanted to try that ice-cap contraption when she heard it was supposed to stop the drug getting to the hair follicles, but one of the other patients told her it hadn't worked for her...just slowed it down and made her look like a dog with mange.'

Even as she laughed at the description Maggie

grimaced. 'Some people think A and E is too stressful but I couldn't work all day with children,' she admitted. 'They're being put through the torments of hell and they're just so stoic and brave that I'd be breaking my heart every day.'

'Well, anyone who wants to find out how stoic and brave Tash is feeling today is welcome to follow me,' Libby invited, suddenly anxious to get back to her daughter's side. If she didn't have to keep working just to keep a roof over their heads, she'd willingly spend every minute with Tash to help to keep her spirits up.

Nick's laughter reached her before she even got as far as the doorway, his deep voice the perfect counterpoint to Tash's sweet giggles.

'You're a rotten cheat, Natasha Cornish! You're not supposed to attack me without warning,' he accused, setting Tash off again so that she was hardly able to use the game controls. Then he caught sight of Libby and her retinue. 'You didn't warn me that this girl is half-shark,' he complained. 'She's beaten me at every turn. My ego is shattered.'

Maggie's expression was so comical that it was obvious to Libby that she'd never expected to see her illustrious colleague in such a situation.

And yet she couldn't see why Maggie should be so surprised. Nick was very good with their young patients in A and E, somehow finding a way to gain their trust even if he was having to do unspeakable things to them. In fact, now that she thought about it, it wasn't that much of a stretch to imagine one of A and E's handsomest doctors as a doting father...if he was ever inclined to give up his bachelor status.

Not that it was likely, she reminded herself firmly as that same old yearning tried to surface. If he'd reached his thirties without taking the plunge, he was hardly likely to consider changing just because she'd turned up in his life again. The attraction between them all those years ago had all been on her side.

'I've got some more visitors for you, Tash,' Libby announced, hoping that no one had noticed that she'd probably been standing there with a besotted expression on her face. There was going to be enough gossip when David and Maggie started visiting Tash and everyone realised just how much the child looked like them. They didn't need any more juicy news to chew on, such as the fact that Libby Cornish still had the same crush on Nick Howell that she'd had when they had been med students together.

What mattered most now was that Tash had all the support she needed to get her through this first gruelling round of chemotherapy.

It was another twenty minutes before the staff nurse in charge stood in the doorway and pointedly cleared her throat.

'I don't know what rules there are about visitor numbers in other departments,' she began primly, even though Libby could see that she was having to hide her pleasure at Tash's raised spirits, 'but the last time I looked, a patient was limited to half a football team at a time, *without* any of the thousands of supporters.'

'Don't be cross, Sam. These are all friends of my mum's,' Tash announced as she sat enthroned on her bed with her entourage ranged around her almost like subjects around a princess. 'And now they're my friends, too, and they're going to be visiting me when Mum's working.'

'Well, as long as they behave themselves and don't all arrive at once…' she said with a warning frown that didn't frighten any of them.

'It's about time I got back to my sproglet anyway,' Leah announced, then added for Tash, 'As soon as you're feeling a bit better, you'll have to come for a visit so you can meet Ethan.'

'And Megan,' Maggie added. 'She's just started eating mashed banana so you could help me to feed her.'

'Could I, Mum?' Tash begged eagerly. 'I've never had a baby to play with 'cos you're always working and you've never got enough time to find someone to give you one.'

Libby felt the start of a blush working its way up her throat and into her face and could see out of the corner of her eyes that there were several stifled grins. She couldn't quite bring herself to meet Nick's gaze, not brave enough to see his response.

'As soon as you're over the chemo,' she promised, hoping that the prospect of such a visit would help her to cope with the debilitating side effects of the drugs.

She finally allowed herself to look towards Nick only to discover that he was no longer in the room, then silently berated herself for allowing it to matter when she'd achieved so much today.

She would never have believed, when she'd been steeling herself to set up the meeting with David and Maggie, that everything would go so smoothly or that they would have been so willing to accept both Tash and herself into their circle so easily. Now she just had to keep her fingers crossed that one of them would be a perfect match if Tash should need a donor.

In the meantime, she had another shift to work with a brain that felt as if it was rapidly turning to cotton wool with lack of sleep. Still, with David, Maggie and Leah apparently only too willing to keep Tash company, she should soon be able to catch up with herself. All she had to do today was concentrate hard and double-check everything she did...

* * *

'Dammit, bitch! I *told* you that hurt!' snarled the drunken lout as he slammed Libby one-handed against the wall.

Libby's head was ringing with the force of the contact and she felt nausea rise in her throat even before her assailant breathed sour fumes into her face.

'I *told* you I needed something for the pain,' he slurred, the hand gripping her neck tightening threateningly as he shook her, banging her head repeatedly as though to reinforce his message.

And then suddenly he was gone and she was sliding down the wall as her legs buckled underneath her, her eyes fixed blankly on the scene playing out in front of her.

'You. Out!' Nick ordered in a voice that brooked no argument, his long fingers wrapped around a meaty arm as he directed her assailant towards the corridor.

'What?' The drunk blinked stupidly as he dug his heels in. 'I'm not going nowhere and you can't make me,' he added belligerently. 'I'm here for treatment to this.' He stuck out the other meaty arm to display the ragged gash left in his arm by a broken bottle.

'Well, you won't be getting it here,' Nick declared firmly as he gestured for the arriving security guards to come into the cubicle to remove the troublemaker.

'I ain't going nowhere until I've had my treatment,' he shouted. 'She's a doctor. She's *got* to treat me.'

'No, she doesn't. Not when you've assaulted her,' Nick countered with steel in every word. 'You're going to have to wait until a male doctor is available, and then only when the police are here to keep an eye on you.'

'Police? It ain't got nothing to do with the police. They weren't here. They didn't see nothing so it's only your word against mine,' he sneered.

'No, but the closed circuit TV saw everything,' Nick countered with a gesture towards the ubiquitous cameras. 'And the police will be able to use the tape when you're brought up in front of a magistrate for assault.'

The man swore crudely, cursing Nick's ancestry and the hospital for having the CCTV system.

'Anyway, it was her own fault,' he accused, gesturing angrily towards Libby as she leaned against the wall. She flinched, her legs barely holding her upright they were trembling so much. 'I told her it hurt and I told her I needed something to take the pain away and all she did was poke and prod it about.'

'To find out whether you'd severed any nerves,' Nick snapped impatiently. 'She was trying to make sure that you weren't going to lose the use of your fingers before she numbed it to do the repair.'

To the security guards, each now holding firmly onto an arm to stop the man flailing about, he said, 'Find out if the relatives' room is free. If not, you'll have to sit on him in Reception till the police get here. Whatever you do, don't let him out of your sight—we don't want any more injuries.'

'Do you want us to send someone in for Dr Cornish?' one of them offered.

'There's no need. I'll take care of her myself,' Nick said, and Libby barely restrained a whimper.

Did it have to be *Nick* who had come to her rescue? She felt so stupid for letting the man blindside her. If she hadn't been so tired she would have been able to anticipate what he was going to do and...

'How badly did he hurt you?' Nick demanded as he wrapped a supportive arm around her shoulders and led her to the nearest chair. This time she couldn't stifle the moan of pleasure that he was handling her so tenderly.

'Did he break any ribs?' he asked as he bent to run exploratory fingers over the thin cotton of her scrubs.

That was more contact than she could bear while she was on emotional overload.

'Just my head and my throat,' she said hastily to forestall any further examination, and put her hand up to the throbbing lump already appearing on the back of her head. 'I hit the wall and then he put his hand around my neck and squeezed.'

'You're going to have bruises,' he said, scowling darkly as he ran gentle fingertips over the abused skin of her throat, and this time the contact sent shivers of pleasure down her spine instead of pain.

'I'll be all right,' she murmured, refusing to allow herself to wallow in his attention and surprised that her voice sounded so normal. 'There's no permanent damage done,' she added as she tried to get to her feet. Unfortunately, her knees weren't co-operating yet.

'You stay right there until I've finished checking you over,' he ordered gruffly. But when he crouched beside her it wasn't to check her eyes for signs of concussion but to ask with every appearance of distress, 'Are you sure you're all right, Libby?'

Her heart missed a beat but she couldn't honestly accept his concern without owning up to her share of the blame.

'It would never have happened if I was concentrating properly,' she admitted dismally.

She saw his mouth tighten as though he was having to bite back the words of condemnation that she deserved. He could probably guess just how little sleep she'd had since Tash's diagnosis.

'It doesn't matter whether you were concentrating or not,' he snapped. 'There's *no* excuse for anyone attacking one of my staff.'

One of my staff. For just a moment she'd hoped he was going to say something personal, that he cared about *her*.

'Having said that,' he continued firmly, 'unless you get some more sleep, you're a liability to the department and you'll be endangering patients. So, get your things together, pay a quick visit to Tash to reassure yourself that she's got plenty of company and go home.'

'But I can't just—'

'You can,' he broke in. 'And don't come back until you've had at least eight hours' uninterrupted sleep,' he ordered, totally ignoring her half-hearted objections.

'But, Nick...'

'Libby, you're not thinking clearly,' he said softly, startling her by taking her hand in his. 'I don't mean that just because of your lack of sleep today, but because you haven't thought about what's going to happen when Tash finishes the chemo. She's going to need you to be firing on all cylinders, not half-dead with exhaustion, and you can't do that without giving your batteries time to recharge.'

'Well, I know that, but—'

'I think it's time for you to admit that you can't do it all by yourself,' he urged. 'I know you haven't been in the area long enough to have developed a large circle of friends, but… what about Tash's father? Shouldn't he be taking some of the burden off your shoulders?'

'Tash is *not* a burden!' she declared through gritted teeth, resenting even the suggestion that she might view her precious daughter in such a way. 'And how I take care of my daughter is none of your business.'

What an idiot she was! For a few moments she'd actually thought that Nick's concern for her was personal, that he might have been about to offer his own time.

'It *is* my business if it compromises your

work,' he said firmly, infuriatingly unruffled. 'And I'm giving you fair warning that if you don't sort something out so that you get a reasonable amount of sleep, I'll have to suspend you until you do.'

'Suspend me?' she squeaked in shock, wondering how she could ever have been so smitten by this bully of a man. He was threatening everything she'd worked for, and without her job... 'You can't! I've got rent to pay and—'

'So you'd better use your time today to get your life organised, or pay the consequences,' he said grimly. 'Is there a good reason why Tash can't spend some time with her father?'

'Only the fact that he's never been part of her life,' she snapped, strangely uncomfortable about having to resort to the usual line she used when people asked.

'Your choice or his?'

'Does it make any difference?' she challenged.

'Only that Tash is a smashing kid and she deserves to know that both her parents want her treatment to succeed.'

'Yes, well, in a perfect world…' She allowed the words to die away, unable to be flippant, not about something that still had the power to plunge her into deep depression if she allowed it to.

He was silent for so long that she was forced to look at him and was surprised to see sympathy rather than condemnation in his expression.

Nick's eyes were bluer than ever as he met her gaze and she could tell that the keen mind behind them was trying to analyse every possible reason why she and Tash's father couldn't co-operate even under such extreme circumstances. The fact that he was kind enough not to voice a single one of them was such a relief that for the first time in a very long time she was almost tempted to tell him the whole sordid story.

Almost.

'So, when *is* your next shift? The day after tomorrow? Well, that should give you enough time to get yourself organised or we'll have to look at cutting your hours,' he finished briskly, and his high-handedness destroyed any chance that she would open her heart to him any time in the next thousand years.

CHAPTER SEVEN

THE faces were grinning at her, surrounding her with their mouths wide open and distorted into manic laughter as they jostled her and bullied her out of the noise of the brightly lit room and into the damp darkness of a winter street.

She tried to scream but nobody seemed to hear her over the driving beat of the music. Who would have taken any notice among the shrill laughter of the groups of people spilling out onto the pavements towards the end of a busy Saturday night? Far too many of them were the worse for wear with drink and high spirits, especially tonight, when they were celebrating the fact that they'd reached the halfway point in their arduous training.

'What'ya got, then?' demanded one of her tor-

mentors, his hands roughly pawing at her and making her wish she'd taken the time to put on her ugly winter coat... But she hadn't wanted to put the dowdy, serviceable thing on tonight, not when she was going to be meeting...

'Nice melons!' leered another as he grabbed a double handful, and she was so shocked by the unexpected assault that she only started to fight in earnest when a third started tugging at her clothing.

''Ere, watch out or she'll get away!' growled a voice as she began to punch and kick at anything that came near her.

Hands kept grabbing at her...more and more hands...tearing at her clothes, at her hair... pulling her down to the ground to subdue her then losing their grip as she fought with renewed terror...

She lost count of the number of times she tried to fight them off, trapped in a nightmare world of fear until suddenly she seemed to break free and terror had her running...running for her life, not caring how far or how fast as long as it took her away from that awful dark place and into the light where she could find some help. And then she found the light...bright, bright light...so bright that it blinded her to the fact that it was bearing down on her and there was no way she could avoid it or it could avoid her...

'No-o-o!' Libby keened, her heart nearly pounding its way out of her chest as she tried to run away from the light, but she couldn't move.

She opened her eyes wide but she couldn't see where to run...couldn't stop the light from...

The light? What light? It was dark. Pitch dark.

'What happened to the light?' she whispered as she fought to sit up in the darkness, her over-sized T-shirt plastered to her sweat-slick body and the bedclothes wrapped around her as though she'd been mummified in her sleep.

She was sure that she'd turned the light on before she'd gone to bed because she hated the dark. Had done ever since...ever since *that* night.

It was actually a relief to have Tash sharing her room because it gave her an excuse for leaving a night-light on; it was logical not to want to wake her daughter by blundering around in the dark. But even though they rarely happened now, her deeper concern had always been that she'd frighten Tash if going to bed in the dark triggered a nightmare.

But this…now…tonight…was the most detailed and the most terrifying the dream had ever been.

The darkness felt like a living presence in the room with her, malevolent, heavy, pressing down on her until it felt as if there wasn't enough oxygen left in the world to fill her lungs and stop her heart beating its way out of her throat.

It took several rasping, gasping breaths before she realised that there was plenty of air to breathe and that her inability to move was easily remedied by unwinding the sheet from around her trembling body.

The one thing that finally allowed the adrenaline to drain from her system was when she reached out to fumble with the light switch, the sudden flood of brightness reaching every corner to reassure her that she was totally alone in the room.

'Why?' she moaned as she slumped back against her battered pillow. 'Why have the nightmares come back? Why now?'

It could hardly be at a worse time, with all her energies divided between Tash and her job. She didn't have any reserves to spare for reliving the terrors that were nearly a decade old.

She peered wearily at the clock, wondering whether there was any point in trying to get to sleep again. She was so tired, and the possibility of being able to catch up on some of the hours she'd missed was a luxury she couldn't afford to waste, but she really didn't think she could cope if the nightmare returned as soon as she closed her eyes.

Nick would probably have something to say if she turned up for her next shift just as exhausted as she'd left. She could just imagine the expression on his face when he caught sight of the dark shadows under her eyes and…

She sighed, picturing the scowl he usually wore

when he looked in her direction, then suddenly re-membered the laughter that had lit his face when he'd been teasing Tash over their computer battle.

Her heart gave an extra thump, the way it always had when she'd caught sight of him at the other side of a lecture theatre or on the other side of a patient's bed, and especially when she'd seen him laughing with the other students in their group. It had filled her with the usual mixture of pleasure at his happiness and sadness that he would never share it with her.

Still, he would never have to know that she'd gone to sleep more than once with impossibly romantic images inside her head of the two of them side by side, walking, talking, kissing, loving...

But, none of that mattered now.

The only thing that mattered was Tash, and if taking advantage of other people's willingness to keep her entertained would help *her* to do the job that put a roof over their heads... So, she would do what she'd always had to do—she would make the best of the situation and just get on with her life, minute by minute.

And if, in those drowsy moments before sleep finally claimed her, she allowed her thoughts to drift into the fantasy of having Nick sharing her bed, his arms wrapped around her as they drifted off together…well, that was strictly between her and her dreams.

If only…Nick mused as he watched Tash sleep, her body seeming impossibly fragile in the wide expanse of the hospital bed.

There really wasn't any reason for him to be there. She'd finally fallen asleep some time ago, worn out by nausea as well as the second-round replay of their computer battles, and she probably wouldn't wake for hours yet.

Still, there was something so valiant about her…something that called to him on an emotional level and made him realise what was missing from his own life…something that actually made him wonder if he could find the courage to risk his heart again.

It took him a moment to subdue the automatic knee-jerk reaction against that thought. It had been happening for nearly a decade and was so habitual that he'd been accepting it as a fact of life. All he'd had to do if he felt himself becoming more than usually attracted to a woman was think of Libby Cornish and any thoughts of allowing a relationship to deepen had vanished instantly.

Except...

Except, now that he'd met her again and was learning more about the person she'd become in the last ten years, aversion was the last thing he was feeling towards Libby Cornish.

She was certainly turning into a good A and E doctor—probably better than he had been at the same stage of his career—and she was already well thought of and popular in the department. As for her abilities as a mother...well, no one could fault her there.

He allowed himself a brief smile at the memory of her glare when he'd issued his ultimatum earlier, but it *had* been necessary because she was obviously quite willing to jeopardise her own health to be there for her daughter.

What wasn't so obvious was why he'd felt so

responsible for making sure she took care of herself, too.

After all that had happened between them, her welfare shouldn't have mattered any more to him than that of any other member of the department...but it did.

He closed his eyes in the subdued lighting of the room as the realisation swept over him in spite of all his determination.

He *shouldn't* care about Libby, not after the way she'd treated him, but somehow that didn't seem to matter any more. He only had to look at her...no, he only had to *think* of her and he...

Tash whimpered, breaking into his increasingly X-rated thoughts, and he was startled to feel a wash of heat working its way up over his cheeks in the gloom.

He stifled a chuckle at the incongruity of it— that someone with a reputation as a bit of a playboy was blushing at the idea that he was thinking about his physical attraction to the mother of the child sleeping in front of him.

But...somehow it was easier to be honest

with himself in such a place, a place where everything was brought down to the essential basics of life and death. And honesty demanded that he admit to himself that he was physically attracted to Libby, as strongly as ever.

Not that she was the same Libby Cornish that he'd known ten years ago. In fact, in some ways she couldn't be more different, now that he really thought about it.

Then she'd been on the plump side with long dark hair that was so shiny that it was always escaping from the tight restraints she tried to put on it. And she'd been so painfully shy, barely daring to make eye contact with her fellow students as she'd hidden in the shadowy corners of whatever room they had been in, soaking information up like a sponge.

Now? Well, she might almost be another person in some ways. The puppy fat was long gone, revealing the stunning slender frame that had hidden beneath. Unfortunately, so was the waterfall of dark hair, but her new, shorter style seemed to accentuate the gleams of copper hidden in its thickness as well as drawing attention to those unforgettable blue-green eyes and the delicate bones of her face.

And her shyness?

This time it was harder to stifle the snort of laughter, especially when he replayed all the times she'd lifted that little pointed chin in his direction and glared her defiance at him.

Obviously, having a child was bound to be a life-changing event, but these were other more fundamental changes to the character he'd known. His shy little plump mouse had certainly come out of the shadows with a vengeance, and every change that he discovered only made him want to learn more about her and about what had happened in the last few years to cause those changes.

Because one thing was certain, he realised as he finally sketched a wave towards the member of staff at the dimly lit desk on his way out of the department, there were dark shadows lurking in Libby's eyes when no one was looking, and something inside him cared deeply enough to want to banish them for her.

'But what are the chances that she'd let me?' he mused aloud in the dubious privacy of the on-call room, somewhere he only had a chance to use in the rare event that there was a lull in the small hours of a quiet night shift.

Then he focused on the wealth of images of Libby inside his head...with all her maternal hackles raised as she realised that there was nothing she could do to ease her daughter's misery...with that intense expression of concentration on her face as she fought for her patients in the department...as wary as an injured doe surrounded by ravenous wolves when anything personal was raised...

He gave a wry chuckle before answering his own question. 'What are your chances of playing the White Knight? Slim to none, mate! Shy little Libby is definitely her own woman now, and will be determined to solve her own problems.'

So, that left him...where? On the outside, looking in?

He paused for a moment, startled when he realised that, in spite of his social popularity, *that* was exactly where he'd always been...where he'd always *wanted* to be...except with Libby. She was the only one who'd been able to slip under his guard while he'd been concentrating on his studies, and in spite of what had happened nearly eight years ago, she'd done it again.

'So, what are you going to do about it? What do you *want* to do about it?' he challenged himself, glad that no one in the department could hear him having this conversation with himself. If they didn't immediately ship him up for an extended visit in the psychiatric unit, they'd definitely be nosy enough to want to know who he was agonising about.

He had a fleeting image of Tash as he'd seen her tonight, whimpering in her sleep, and felt the answering tug on his heart strings. She was a smashing kid who really didn't deserve the hell she was going through and...and who *could* be the answer to his dilemma, he realised with a flash of inspiration.

He lay very still, almost afraid to take that idea to its logical conclusion, but it certainly bore some consideration.

He wouldn't be *using* Tash to get to her mother because he genuinely liked the sparky youngster for herself and enjoyed spending time with her...even if she was getting far too close for his liking to beating him on the computer *without* his assistance.

He also still had to come to terms with the fact that she wasn't his daughter, but she and Libby were a package deal and if he and Libby...then Tash would become...

He was definitely getting ahead of himself.

He was vaguely aware that his thoughts were drifting and shredding...becoming tangled in the threads of sleep that were dragging him down into the darkness...but for the first time in a very long time he felt warm inside and that brought a lingering ghost of a smile to his face.

'You're looking better!'

Libby's heart leapt when Nick's was the first

voice she heard when she walked into the department for her next shift.

She turned and grimaced at him, determined that he wouldn't guess that her pulse rate had doubled and all her hormones were singing the 'Halleluiah Chorus' at their first sight of him.

'Considering how washed-out I still look, that's a dubious compliment,' she grumbled. 'Until I slept for fourteen hours straight through, I hadn't realised just how tired I was.'

'Exhausted,' he agreed, far too quickly for her liking. 'Do you need a few minutes to visit Tash before you start your shift?'

'I've just come from her.' Libby smiled but knew there was a wry edge to it. 'She was telling me about all the visitors she's had in the last couple of days. She barely seemed to have realised that I hadn't been there.'

'She knew,' he said softly, the expression in his eyes reassuring her. 'She told me that you were very tired and would come back when you woke up. She knows she can trust you,' he added, and her heart swelled at his perception, that he'd told her the one thing she'd really needed to hear.

'Thank you for that,' she whispered, half-afraid that she was going to embarrass herself by bursting into tears all over him. She swallowed hard and drew in a steadying breath. 'So, has the department survived without me?' she quipped.

'Only just. There was no one free to make me a cup of coffee when I woke up from my snooze in the on-call room, so I had to get it myself,' he teased, just as the familiar ring tone of the red phone in Reception shrilled, the direct connection to the ambulance station a warning of something serious on the way in.

'Look at that!' he grumbled even as she had to hurry to keep up with his much longer strides. 'You must be a jinx. You've hardly been inside the door a couple of minutes and our peaceful existence is shattered. What have we got, Kelly?' he demanded before the senior nurse had a chance to put the receiver down.

'RTA times three,' she said succinctly. 'Some plonker driving at speed, the wrong way along a dual carriageway, so the other cars were swerving all over the place to try to avoid going head on with him.'

'And colliding with everyone else,' Nick finished for her. 'How many victims and how severe?'

'Seven, so far, but with the police still in pursuit, that could rise. And there's everything from whiplash and cuts from flying glass to someone trapped inside a car that flipped onto its roof.'

'*Hell!*' he swore with feeling, voicing Libby's thoughts exactly. 'Well, we've done it before and we all know what to do,' he said, raising his voice to be heard over the usual hubbub of the busy department to call the troops to order. 'Depending what chaos they find on scene, the paramedics will have done triage before they deliver to us, but we still need someone to check the priorities as they come in the door. Libby, will you have a word with the patients waiting for attention in Minors? Make certain that they understand that—'

'That their waiting times will probably stretch

into infinity,' she interrupted briskly. 'Will do.' She turned and hurried to the waiting area at the minor injuries end of the department, already dreading the reaction she was going to get from some of the people there. Behind her, she could hear the other members of staff being detailed to check that their posts were completely ready for the imminent influx of injuries.

'Unfortunately, sir, it's a fact of life that a hospital can't work on a first-come, first-served basis. Patients with life-threatening injuries will always have to be treated first,' she reiterated for the umpteenth time, this time to the irate man with the nail torn halfway off his thumb during botched DIY. 'Your pain relief will be renewed if it wears off before you can be seen, but I can only repeat that you'll be seen as soon as there's someone free to see you and that I have no idea how long that will be. You could always phone your GP's surgery to see if they could fit you in sooner. Lots of them have the basic facilities to deal with minor surgical procedures like yours. Now, if you'll excuse me...'

Libby gestured towards the rows of plastic chairs, silently suggesting that he take a seat.

To her relief, he did, but not without some heavy-duty muttering under his breath as he went. To her further relief, Kelly was beckoning her across, signalling her escape from her current thankless task.

'We need you in Majors,' Kelly said firmly when she joined her in the corridor, and Libby found herself once again having to scurry along in the wake of a longer-legged companion.

'In my next life, I'm coming back as a stork or a giraffe,' she muttered crossly, then yelped in alarm when she nearly ploughed into Kelly's back as she halted in mid-stride.

'What was that?' the senior sister demanded, eyes wide with disbelief.

'You weren't supposed to hear, but I said, "In my next life, I'm coming back as a stork or a giraffe,"' Libby grumbled.

'What? Why?' Kelly was clearly so bemused at the thought that Libby couldn't help chuckling.

'Because they've got long legs!' she said with

feeling. 'You wouldn't believe how frustrating it is to have to run to keep up with everybody.'

'You've made my day!' Kelly laughed as she took off again, this time a little slower. 'I'm not so tall myself, and that's the first time I've ever been told my legs are too long. Now, let's get our little legs moving. There are patients to see and Nick needs your help.'

Her first glance inside Resus One, where Nick was working, told Libby that Kelly hadn't been exaggerating.

'Where do you want me?' she offered as she swiftly donned a disposable apron and pulled on a fresh pair of gloves.

'You can help me find out where all this blood is coming from,' Nick growled, clearly frustrated. 'I'm on my own with it until one of the surgeons is free and that could be hours.'

'You haven't *got* hours,' warned the anaesthetist. 'His BP is plummeting so you'd better find out fast.'

Without having to be told, Libby positioned herself to take over the task of suctioning the blood from the operating field, trying to keep herself and the tool as much as possible out of Nick's way as he meticulously checked each of his patient's internal organs for damage, all the while muttering incomprehensibly under his breath.

Over his head she gestured for one of the nurses to set up another bag of fluid, grateful for the delivery of matched blood that arrived just at the right moment.

The monitors were screaming out their deafening warnings of imminent danger and she'd just mimed for the bags to be manually squeezed to speed up the rate of delivery when Nick spoke.

'At last!' he exclaimed. 'Gotcha!' The next few minutes were a flurry of clamps and sutures, interspersed with apparently blood-curdling Russian profanities as he fought to repair the damage and get the bleeding under control before they lost the fight.

Libby had never seen anyone tie sutures so fast or so accurately, especially under pressure, and when the clamps were taken off and there wasn't so much as a hint of a leak she couldn't help the beam of pride and delight that spread over her face.

'How's his pressure now?' she asked, hardly needing to hear the figures to know that Nick had pulled it off.

'On the way back up,' the anaesthetist reported, relief clear in his voice. 'It won't be long before he's stable enough to be transferred up to Theatre.'

'That's all well and good if there's a theatre free,' Nick pointed out darkly. 'If not, he'll need closing down here, and there are patients still waiting to be seen.'

He was clearly torn, and the least Libby could do was take her courage in both hands and some of the load off his shoulders.

'I could close for you, if you trust me...to let you get on to the next one,' she offered.

The pause was less than a heartbeat, even as it sent her own heart into her throat while she waited for his reply.

'Of course I trust you,' he said quietly, those

incredible blue eyes unwavering as he met her gaze. 'But give me a shout if you need me. I won't be far away. OK?'

'OK,' she agreed, feeling almost as if she could have walked on water in that moment.

In front of a room full of colleagues, Nick had said he trusted her to take over his patient, but in his eyes there had been something more… something deeper…going on.

Now wasn't the best time to think about it, with a patient's precarious state of health depending on her skill to finish what Nick had started, but once the emergency situation was over…

'Right, I need some suction here,' she said quietly as she gathered her thoughts and turned her concentration to the job in hand. She had a great deal of careful stitching to do if she was to minimise the patient's likelihood of developing serious adhesions. There was no point in saving his life if it was going to be a misery as the result of botched stitchery.

It was nearly three hours before any of them drew a deep breath.

The carnage had continued arriving until the perpetrator himself had arrived at the accident department, closely followed by the policeman whose car he had rammed at high speed in a final failed attempt at evading capture.

Nothing had actually been said, but there was an air of grim satisfaction in the room when they heard that, in spite of two broken legs, the policeman would probably be able to return to normal life, even though his assailant wouldn't. In fact, it was unlikely that he would survive the night.

'Well done, troops!' Nick said as he came into the room an hour later bearing a large white box with the name of a nearby bakery along the side. 'Grab yourselves some calories,' he invited as he set the opened box on the nearest table to reveal an assortment of doughnuts, some with the traditional coating of sugar and others with icing or chocolate.

In an instant the whole group that had been sprawled about in various poses of complete exhaustion came to life, leaping to their feet to descend on the offered treats like so many locusts.

'Aren't you going to have one?' Nick asked when he caught sight of Libby making for the door.

'Actually, I was thinking of taking my break upstairs with Tash,' Libby said diffidently, wondering at Nick's changed attitude towards her.

It hadn't been so long ago that he'd been glaring at her at every opportunity. Today, he'd not only complimented her medical skills in front of their colleagues but he almost seemed to be seeking her company.

'Does Tash like doughnuts?'

'Is the sky blue?' she countered with a grin, remembering the contests the two of them had, trying to eat a whole sugared doughnut without licking their lips. 'If she'd seen that boxed assortment…!'

'Which ones are her favourite?' It was his turn to smile and his eyes seemed to gleam a brighter blue.

'Her absolute favourites are chocolate.' It was hard to find breath for conversation when he was standing so close.

'And yours?'

'Traditional, with jam in the middle.'

'Well, then, I've got the perfect selection,' he announced as he pushed the door open with his shoulder and gestured for her to lead the way with the hand that now held a much smaller version of the rapidly emptying bakery box in the room behind them.

'A selection…of what?' Her tongue stumbled over the words when she felt his hand settle at the small of her back as he ushered her into the lift.

'Doughnuts,' he said patiently, as though the answer should have been obvious, then he smiled that million-dollar smile that doubled her heartbeat in a nanosecond and totally removed any semblance of strength or co-ordination in her knees. 'I thought that—provided we don't get anything major coming in for the next few minutes—we could both go up and share them with Tash.'

CHAPTER EIGHT

THIS isn't working, said a voice inside Libby's head.

It was the same insidious voice that had accompanied every one of her vigils beside Tash's bed, the one that had questioned, endlessly, *What if this doesn't work?*

Every time the next dose of chemotherapy was administered, she found herself superstitiously crossing her fingers, and every time samples were taken for testing, she prayed while she waited for the results.

Now it looked as if all the crossed-fingers and prayers had been in vain because the results weren't anything like what Doug Andrews had told her he was looking for by this stage.

And still she couldn't bring herself to say anything, as though by voicing her doubts she would be making them true. All she'd been able to concentrate on was the day-by-day and minute-by-minute things that she had to do, such as work her assigned shifts in A and E, shop, cook, do laundry and spend as much time with Tash as she could, as if, by never allowing herself to look up to see the larger picture, she could somehow prevent anything bad from happening.

That wasn't going to work much longer, not now that Doug had specifically asked her to come up to see him. She knew, in her heart of hearts, that all the *should* and *might* and *maybe* was going to come to an end. He was going to tell her that the chemotherapy hadn't worked and...

'Libby!'

The sharp tone in Nick's voice not only dragged her out of her spiral of black despairing thoughts but also told her that it wasn't the first time he'd spoken to her.

'I'm sorry. What were you saying?' For a moment she was ready to panic that he had another patient for her to see, even though she'd told him the time of her meeting with Doug Andrews. Much as she was dreading it, she couldn't possibly miss that appointment. Tash's life could depend on it.

'I was saying,' he said patiently, 'that it's time to go up for the meeting with Doug. You don't want to be late.'

'What *is* the time, then?' She glanced around wildly, completely forgetting for a panicky moment that there was a large clock on the wall in the reception area.

'Time to go,' he reiterated as he held out one hand towards her. 'Come on.'

She'd clung on to that hand like a drowning swimmer to a lifeline before she realised what she was doing.

'Where are *you* going?' she demanded, trying to pull her hand away again but he wouldn't release her.

'I'm coming with you,' he declared as he ushered her into the lift that always seemed to be waiting just when he wanted it. 'Unless you've got any objection?'

'Objection?' she parroted blankly. At the moment, with fear turning her brain to mush, she'd be hard-pressed to remember her name let alone formulate any sort of debate.

'Right. Let's make this simple,' he said with a sigh, then deliberately turned to face her, lifting her chin with a gentle finger until her eyes met his. 'Would you like me to come with you while you have your meeting with Doug?'

The tender caring in the suggestion brought the threat of tears to her eyes.

'Yes, please,' she whispered. 'I've been dreading it all day.'

'As if I couldn't tell,' he said in a teasing voice. 'How many sugars *did* you put in my tea, by the way?'

'I don't know,' she admitted with an answering grin, remembering his disgusted expression when he'd taken that first mouthful. 'And I've no idea why I put *any* in, considering that I know you don't take sugar.'

'I rest my case,' he said smugly, and then they were there and it was time to step out of the lift and walk along the corridor to Doug's room and…

'Take a deep breath and put one foot in front of the other,' Nick murmured in her ear, the soft puff of his warm breath sending a totally inappropriate shiver along her spine, but at least it momentarily took her mind off the ordeal that faced her in just a few minutes.

'Libby. Nick. Come in and make yourselves comfortable,' Doug invited, and Libby filed away for future consideration the fact that he really wasn't in the least surprised to see Nick with her. The only thing that mattered now was…

'It's not working, is it?' she said bluntly, then closed her eyes and shook her head at her loss of control. 'I'm sorry, but…'

'Don't apologise,' Doug said kindly, his expression sombre. 'Because you're right, up to a point.'

'"Up to a point!" What do you mean "up to a point"? Tash isn't responding to the chemo. It's a complete failure,' she accused, then slapped a hand over her unruly mouth and started apologising all over again.

'Hush, Libby. Gently,' Nick said, taking her hand in his and threading their fingers together before cradling his other hand over the top. 'Let the man speak.'

'I'm sorr—' She swallowed the rest when he tightened his fingers around hers and subsided, uncertain how she came to be plastered quite so closely to Nick's side but very grateful for that closeness.

'As I was saying, the cocktail of drugs we tried for this first round of chemo didn't do a good enough job, so, as Tash isn't much further forward, I'm proposing changing the mix completely and starting the next course straight away.'

Libby was torn. One half of her motherly instincts wanted to grab the suggestion with both hands—anything to save her daughter's life—but the other half, the half that had suffered through every minute of the debilitating nausea with her daughter, desperately didn't want her to have to go through the whole thing again without a break.

Then, of course, there was the ultimate question.

'And what do we do if she doesn't respond to *this* mixture of drugs either?' she demanded, everything suddenly overwhelming her. 'Will you run a third course until she's completely exhausted? She's only eight, for heaven's sake. She's just a little girl. She's supposed to be out playing with her friends, not in here fighting for her life when she can't even keep food down.'

It wasn't until Nick passed her a handful of paper hankies from the box on the table beside him that she realised that, apart from screaming at the senior oncology specialist in the hospital, she also had tears streaming down her face.

'I know,' Doug said quietly, sadly, and rubbed both hands wearily over his face. 'Believe me, I know. I lost my son to leukaemia. My own son, and I couldn't do anything to save him.'

The sombre silence of shared misery stretched out until Nick broke it.

'Where are we with finding a match for a bone-marrow donor? Was there a good enough match within the family?' Of necessity, they'd had to explain the hidden relationship between

Tash and the ffrench family, although the information wasn't generally known.

Doug was silent for a worrying moment before he spoke. 'I would hope that we could find a better match than either of them if it comes to needing a bone-marrow graft,' he said finally. 'I would hate to think we had to work with something that wasn't as perfect a match as possible.'

It felt as if a huge hole had opened up in Libby's chest where her heart should be.

She'd been so relieved when David and Maggie had agreed so readily to be tested, certain that she had every eventuality covered to ensure that Tash would soon be well. To find out that *neither* of them was a good enough match was a blow she hadn't anticipated.

Terror slowed her thought processes so far that it felt as if she was trying to follow the rest of the conversation underwater.

All she could remember by the time Nick was ushering her back out into the corridor was that the decision had been made to start Tash on the next round of chemo in the morning.

Her feet automatically started to take her in the direction of Tash's room and the urge to snatch her precious daughter out of her hospital bed and run as far and as fast as she could was almost irresistible. Libby actually tried to fight him when Nick led her into the little lounge used for conferences between family members and staff, but then he pushed the door closed and stood with his back against it.

She knew from the determined expression on his face that he had something he wanted to say and there was nothing she could do but give in to the inevitable.

'What?' she snapped, her fists planted belligerently on her hips. 'So, I was rude to Doug Andrews when he's only doing his best? OK. I'll apologise, even though I doubt I said anything he hasn't heard from dozens of parents...hundreds, even. *Now* can I go and see my daughter?'

'I don't care if you hurl abuse at every doctor on the staff if it helps you to cope with what you're going through,' he said quietly, and completely took the wind out of her sails. It also left her completely baffled about his reason for hijacking her on her way to see Tash.

'Well, if that isn't what you wanted to talk about, why have you barricaded me in here?'

'Because there's something I don't understand, something I need to know…for Tash's sake,' he added almost as an afterthought.

'What?' Libby had felt bad about the way she'd treated the oncologist, knowing he was doing his best to help Tash, and her guilt had made her defensive enough to snap at Nick when she'd thought he was taking her to task.

This was obviously something entirely different and suddenly she didn't have a good feeling about where this conversation might be going.

'Libby, you heard what Doug said just now,' he began in a slightly uneasy preamble that sent a shiver of apprehension up her spine. Nick *never* beat about the bush if he had something to say. 'They've had the results back on David and Maggie and they don't match well enough as potential donors to be any help to Tash.'

'Yes, Nick. I was there. I heard what he said and

I know how serious it is,' she said, once more having to fight the feeling of panic that time might be running out. There was always another desperate last-minute plea by distraught parents for people to come forward to be tested. Would it be Tash's face staring out from the television screens next?

'So, if you realise the seriousness of the situation, why haven't you contacted Tash's father to ask him to be tested?' he demanded fiercely. 'Surely you can put any bad feeling between the two of you aside for long enough to save your daughter's life!'

Libby felt the blood drain out of her face as his words hit her with the force of a knock-out punch.

Her mother had been the only one who knew the story of Tash's conception, and with her gone, Libby had hoped that what had happened could finally be forgotten…except for the recurring dreams that would never let her forget.

'Don't you think I would if I could?' she spat furiously, tired of living with the ragged, terrible memories and finished with a wail filled with despair. 'But I don't *know*!'

'I don't understand.' Dark blond eyebrows drew together, pleating his forehead in a deep frown. 'You don't know where he is? Just give us the name and the police can probably help us to track him down.'

'If only it *was* that easy!' she said brokenly as she sank onto the arm of the nearest chair, suddenly too weary to remain standing any longer now that she knew she was going to have to tell him everything...well, as much as he needed to know to understand why...

'I don't know who her father is,' she announced abruptly, and only realised how bad that sounded when his eyes widened with surprise. Well, if this conversation changed the way he thought about her, that was something she'd have to deal with later. He knew as well as anyone that she'd never been attractive enough to entertain a string of lovers.

'That accident I told you about...I was attacked,' she said, determined to get the worst over with. 'I don't know how many of them there were because when I ran away I got knocked over and spent some time in a coma. There are parts of my memory that will probably never return, in all likelihood because they're too awful to cope with, but...'

'You were in a coma?' he demanded hoarsely. 'When? Where?'

It was vaguely reassuring that Nick had apparently ignored the emotive issue of the fact that she'd been attacked in favour of wanting details of the medical one.

'You probably didn't notice that I was gone because I wasn't part of your group, but it happened almost exactly halfway through training,' she explained, managing to cope more easily than she'd expected as long as she was only having to give him hard facts. There was a strange expression on his face and he was pressing his lips together in a tight line as though forcing himself to remain silent, but he was definitely concentrating on every word.

'You probably remember that each year there's a group of med students celebrating reaching the halfway point in their training, and they usually meet up for a drink.'

'A drink that usually ends up turning into a pub crawl for the ones who don't have to get up early the next morning,' he supplied wryly.

'Exactly, which is why I have no idea why I decided to go out for a drink that night. I know it just wasn't my scene but I can't remember…'

'How much *do* you remember?' he asked, visibly shaken.

'Of the attack? Far too much, unless the recurring nightmares are all my imagination,' she said with a shudder.

'And how much of that time…how much of your memory have you lost?' he pressed. 'Obviously, there's the time you were in the coma, but how much more is missing? Is it weeks, months…?'

'I've never been able to work it out because my life was such a routine when I was studying,' she admitted, apologetic and almost ashamed to have been so boring. No wonder he'd never noticed her. 'Each day was much like the one before and the one after except for the patients I saw on the wards, and even *they* tended to blur after a while.'

'Especially when you're chronically short of sleep,' he agreed, and she actually felt that he might understand what it had been like. 'But I don't understand why we didn't know that you were in ICU. No one seemed to know where you were when you didn't turn up the next day.'

'That's because I wasn't taken to *our* hospital,' she explained, amazed that he *had* noticed that she'd disappeared. That was an unexpected stroke to her ego after all this time. 'And as I was admitted without any identification, no one had any idea who I was until I came out of the coma.'

'And then?'

'I was waiting to be declared fit to leave hospital and I had organised a meeting with the Dean to see if it would still be possible for me to catch up on the time I'd missed, or whether it would be better if I waited the rest of the year out and resumed my training in the autumn. That's when one of the doctors who'd admitted me sat me down and told me that there had been some sort of mix-up in some tests.'

She shook her head when she remembered how surreal that conversation had been.

'He was almost babbling as he told me that, ordinarily, they'd just have ignored the mix-up and repeated the correct ones, but in the circumstances…bearing in mind what had happened and the fact that my memory wasn't reliable…'

'Et cetera, et cetera.' Nick nodded. 'I've come across doctors like that. Just can't come to the point if they're the bearer of bad news.'

'Then he told me I was pregnant, and that as it was the result of rape, I could ask for an abortion for the sake of my mental well-being.'

'And you said…?'

'That it was possible that I might decide to have it adopted, but the baby was totally innocent of any wrong-doing and I could never commit murder.'

'And he went away with his tail between his legs, suitably chastened,' Nick added with a brief chuckle before his expression grew serious once more. 'I knew something had gone wrong because I've seen the shadows in your eyes, but I never imagined it was anything like this, Libby. I'm sorry I made you go over it again when you must be trying to forget it.'

'I've been reliving it on a nightly basis the last few weeks,' she admitted wearily. 'Look on the bright side—perhaps the fact that I've told you about it will act as some sort of exorcism and I'll be able to sleep the night through.'

'I hope so. You still look woefully short of sleep,' he pointed out bluntly. 'But all that doesn't get us any closer to finding a donor to match Tash,' he added, dragging them both back to the reason for the whole conversation.

Suddenly, the memories of her assault and its aftermath paled into insignificance in comparison with this latest setback to Tash's treatment, and Libby couldn't see any way past it.

'I can't think about that now,' she declared, deliberately forcing the problem to the back of her mind as she stood up. 'Before I go back to work I'm just going to spend a couple of minutes with Tash. I need to talk to her…to prepare her for the fact that she's got to go through the whole miserable thing all over again.'

'Take your time, Libby,' Nick said softly, reaching out a gentle hand to stroke the back of a finger along her cheek. 'I'll have you paged if we get buried under admissions, but at the moment I think you need to spend some time with Tash as much as she needs you.'

'Thank you,' she whispered, leaning into the contact and feeling the warmth of his skin seeping into her soul.

It was pointless to wish that Nick was Tash's father…as pointless as wishing for the moon, she reminded herself as she finally made her way back down to A and E. Her heart was still in Tash's room, aching for the child with the tears still drying on her cheeks as she slept with exhaustion after railing bitterly at the unfairness of life.

Well, her mother had always warned her that life wasn't fair, but she'd hoped her daughter would have a few more years of in-

nocence before she had to learn that unpalat-
able truth.

Now all she could do was start all over again,
keeping her fingers crossed with every dose of
chemotherapy and praying that the next set of
results would be the ones to tell them that the
treatment was finally working.

There was a strange feeling in the air when she
arrived in the department the next morning. It
wasn't quite excitement, but there was definitely something going on.

'Kelly, do you know what's happening?' she
demanded when yet another member of staff
deliberately gave her arm a squeeze, and she'd
only been there for five minutes.

'Ah, well.' Kelly stalled for a moment, almost
as though lost for words. 'I think you'd better
have a word with Nick,' she sidestepped adroit-
ly, and pointed over Libby's shoulder.

'Nick Howell, what on earth's going on
around here?' she demanded when she responded to his invitation to enter the office.

'Kelly told me to come and have a word with you to find out… Oh, my…'

She was speechless when she saw the prototype for a flyer sitting on the corner of the desk.

'I hope you don't mind?' he said with a gesture towards the photo of Tash sitting up in her hospital bed with a wary smile on her face, her gorgeous hair already starting to look a little moth-eaten. 'I took it with a digital camera and put it through my computer. I had every intention of showing it to you to get your permission before I printed it up and posted it up around the hospital, but Kelly caught sight of it and…'

'And now it's all around the hospital courtesy of the grapevine,' she finished for him, so surprised by this sudden turn of events that she didn't know whether to be angry that it had happened without her knowledge or agreement, or to throw her arms around him in gratitude.

'And I just had a phone call from the labs saying they're being swamped by requests to be tested to see if they're a match for her, and they want me to add a line to the flyer giving the proper contact details so the whole system doesn't grind to a halt.'

'They're swamped? Already?' She *definitely* wanted to throw her arms around him. 'In which case, how can I be so petty as to tell you off for taking Tash's photo without permission?'

'I *was* going to tell you…to show you what we'd come up with…'

'We?' she queried with a pang of disappointment, wondering who else he'd roped in to help instead of her.

'Tash and I. She helped me to do the design and choose the typeface…'

'*Tash?*' That was difficult to picture. The last time she'd seen her daughter she had been curled up in a ball, still devastated by the news that she was going to have to start another round of chemotherapy.

'When I went up she was in such a state about the next lot of chemo that… Well, that's partly why I did it in the first place—to give her something else to focus on because she was so down. Mind you, I did warn her that you might put a lid on the whole thing…'

'But then Kelly caught sight of the prototype and the cat was out of the bag.'

'With a vengeance,' he agreed. 'So…are you OK about it? I mean, you're not angry that I took liberties, are you?'

'Angry?' She laughed incredulously. 'I spent hours last night racking my brain for some way to catch people's attention and persuade them to be tested, and I come in this morning to find that you've already grabbed them around the throat with *this*!' She snatched up the flyer and waved it in his face. '"Do it for one of our own",' she read aloud from the words under the photo, her voice choking with emotion. 'How could I possibly be angry when it's already working? I could *kiss* you!'

There was a startled second of surprise as her impulsive words echoed back at her before a wicked grin spread across his face and he opened his arms wide in invitation.

'Feel free,' he said with a gleam of challenge in his eyes.

If it hadn't been for that gleam she would have been able to resist...maybe. But when he was offering something that she'd been fantasising about for more than a decade, it was impossible to resist the temptation...just once.

Except when she took that fateful step forward to place her hands on his shoulders, then had to go up on her toes because, arrogant brute that he was, he was making her do all the work...when she flicked a nervous tongue over her lips then pressed them uncertainly to his, she knew she would never be satisfied with just once.

It felt like coming home, her brain told her as every nerve ending went into overload.

It felt as if she'd kissed him before, not once but many times, and not just in her dreams.

'You dream about me?' Nick asked, and she realised that she'd actually spoken her thoughts aloud.

'Ah-h-h!' she groaned, burying her burning face against his shoulder to hide her flush of embarrassment. 'If you're a gentleman, you'll forget I said that.'

'Forget what will become one of my most treasured memories?' he teased gently. 'No chance!'

'It was ten years ago, when we first met,' she tried to convince him, willing to embarrass her younger self to divert his attention from how she felt now. 'I had a terrible crush on you right from the moment we were registering on the course but, of course, you never even noticed me.'

As he lowered his head to brush his lips over hers it sounded almost as if he whispered, 'I noticed', but that was another of her unlikely fantasies so she had to ignore it. She couldn't do much else when he was teasing her with the lightest of touches and asking, 'Was it worth waiting for or do you need another sample…for clinical analysis?'

'By all means, let us do a thorough clinical analysis,' Libby agreed weakly, her mouth already tingling in anticipation as he took over control of their second kiss.

'Oh! Excuse me!' said a voice at the door, and the two of them sprang apart like guilty adolescents caught out by the teacher.

'Sally!' Libby called when she recognised her friend making a rapid exit. 'Did you need to speak to one of us?'

'I didn't want to intrude,' she said with a hint of mischief in her smile. 'I can come back later, when it's more convenient.'

And in the meantime, she'd be spreading tales about what she'd interrupted, and they'd grow with every re-telling, Libby thought with a sinking heart. And it had all been *her* fault.

'I…I was just thanking Nick. For…for doing the flyer about Tash,' she stumbled, uneasily aware that she was probably making the whole situation worse.

'If you say so,' Sally murmured under her breath, and Libby was so embarrassed that she didn't dare look at Nick to see if he was blushing as hotly as she was. 'I just wanted to pick Nick's brain about the—'

'I'll leave you to it, then,' Libby interrupted

hurriedly, and only just stopped herself running out of the room like a scared rabbit.

It was an hour or two before she calmed down enough to admit that the only thing that prevented the whole episode from being totally humiliating was the fact that Nick's kiss had been everything she'd fantasised about and more.

CHAPTER NINE

LIBBY had no idea what Nick had said to Sally after she'd left the room but, whatever it was, it had worked. Several days had passed since Sally had walked in and found them kissing, but she didn't seem to have told anyone what she'd seen. There hadn't been so much as a hint of gossip about Nick and herself.

Instead, the whole hospital was apparently gripped by the drama started by Nick's flyers about Tash, keeping their fingers crossed that someone, somewhere would volunteer to be tested and would be found to be the perfect match for her.

In A and E alone, several dozen members of staff, from porters and cleaners right up to consultants, had volunteered for testing, a fact that made Libby feel tearful with gratitude every time she thought of it.

In the meantime, Tash's treatment was progressing. This time, thankfully, she seemed to be suffering a little less nausea, but that was more than made up for by the cracked and bleeding lips and a mouthful of painful ulcers.

In spite of her physical misery, her spirits were far higher than Libby had expected, due largely to the constant stream of visitors who kept her company and entertained her.

Nick, in particular, seemed to spend most of his on-call hours with her when the department was quiet enough for him to get away, and as for his off-duty time…for some reason, a large proportion of that seemed to coincide with her own so that she often arrived up on the ward to find him already ensconced at the side of Tash's bed.

'I beat him, Mum! I beat him, fair and square!' she squealed when she caught sight of Libby in the doorway. 'You didn't cheat this time, did you? You weren't deliberately letting me win?'

'Not this time, I wasn't,' he said with a theatrical scowl. 'I was determined not to let you win but there was nothing I could do to stop you. You're getting far too clever.'

'*And* I got a better score than him on the other game, and I did it faster, too,' she boasted, and if it hadn't been for the lurid pink flowered hat that covered her head, hiding the fact that she had very little hair left, Libby could almost think that there was nothing wrong with her precious daughter.

Libby was refusing to allow herself to think about the progress of the treatment this time. She was forcing herself to live in the moment and enjoy every second of the time she spent with Tash, and if that included spending a great deal of that time with Nick, too…well, she certainly wasn't going to complain.

There was definitely something different about the atmosphere between the two of them. She wasn't certain whether it had come about as a result of Nick's willingness to get involved with the flyer campaign to drum up donors. That, in turn, could have been the result of

Libby finally telling him about her coma and the resulting retrograde amnesia, because ever since that fraught conversation, there seemed to have been an extra sparkle in his eyes, and as for that lady-killer smile…

Well, it had always had a devastating effect on her, even when it hadn't been directed at her, and now that it was, and at close quarters, she didn't stand a chance against its potency.

Even here, in Tash's hospital room, he seemed to take advantage of every chance to touch her, put his arm around her or lean over her shoulder, and she was loving every moment.

Best of all, when Tash finally fell asleep tonight, she had the prospect of going out for a meal with Nick, to the little family-run Italian restaurant just along the road from St Luke's. It would be the first time they'd gone out together on anything that resembled a date and seemed to mark the start of a new phase in their relationship. And even though she knew it was highly unlikely that either of them were ready to take things that far tonight, she'd even taken advantage of the fact that he was keeping Tash company to dash off for a quick shower and a change out of her ordinary underwear into something more…

'Ah, Nick!' said a voice from the doorway, dragging her thoughts away from imagining Nick's reaction if he saw her in black satin and lace.

They all turned to see Doug standing there with a strange expression on his face. 'I thought you might be here,' he said with a strangely uneasy glance in Libby's direction. 'Have you got a moment?'

Nick frowned at the unexpected request and, when he met Libby's gaze, shook his head to tell her that he had no idea what it was about.

After he'd disappeared from sight she glanced at her watch and wondered how long it would be before he returned. She didn't like the idea of work intruding on the precious time they spent together.

Still, with Tash still to settle for the night, she had plenty to do to occupy herself until he came back, and then it would be time to go out together for their first time as a couple.

Would it be the first of many, or would Nick gradually return to his playboy ways once Tash was on the mend? She didn't like to think so, not now that he'd started to get so close to her daughter. Tash would be so hurt if the man she'd come to idolise began to ignore her, and if she never saw him again…

As for her own feelings, after so many years of fantasising about him, she'd had a chance to discover that the real man was even more wonderful than she'd imagined and she was fathoms deep in love with him.

They worked together seamlessly in A and E, the two of them anticipating each other's needs almost as though they were reading each other's minds. Even Kelly had noticed how well they got on these days, so much so that she'd started pairing the two of them together to work with the most severe or complicated injuries.

Libby was thriving on the challenge of being thrown in the deep end of such a busy department in that way and was learning so much about emergency medicine, but most of all she was learning exactly how much Nick meant to her and how much a part of her life he had become in such a short time. If anything came between them now, it would break her heart.

'Libby?' He appeared in the doorway as if in answer to her thoughts and her heart threw in a couple of extra beats in anticipation of their evening together. But before she could get to her feet to accompany him out of Tash's room he was shaking his head. 'Libby…I'm sorry. Something's come up. I'm going to have to cancel this evening,' he said shortly, not sounding in the least bit like himself.

'Is there a problem? Anything I can help with?' she offered softly so that she didn't wake Tash now that she was asleep, worried about the strained look on his face. She had no idea what Doug might have needed to discuss with Nick that would have caused a reaction like this, but it was something that had leached all the colour from his face. If she had a chance to talk to him, perhaps he would confide…

'No.' He was abnormally abrupt and seemed almost at a loss for words. 'I'm sorry, Libby, but this is…it's something that I need to sort out myself. I'll…I'll get back to you…' And without even a hint that he might have liked to give her his usual hug goodbye, he was gone.

'Ouch! That looks painful!' Libby exclaimed when she joined her next patient in the curtained cubicle.

'Tell me about it!' the young man muttered, the clarity of his speech severely affected by the angry-looking swelling on his jaw. 'Can't eat…can't speak…can't sleep.'

'So, how long has it been like this?' Libby bent forward to begin a gentle examination, feeling for swollen lymph nodes as she tried to assess whether the swelling was purely affecting soft tissue or whether the jaw bone was involved, too.

'Only a couple of days, but it feels like months. It happened so fast, from a bit of a toothache to this!' he mumbled, then drew in a sharp breath of agony when he tried to open his mouth wide enough to allow her to probe between cheek and teeth.

'Right,' she said as she straightened up. 'I'm almost positive that this is nothing more than a massive abscess, possibly stemming from an underlying dental problem,' she explained.

'You're not going to make me wait for an appointment with my dentist, are you?' he demanded, clearly horrified at the prospect. 'That could take weeks!'

'I wouldn't be so cruel,' Libby reassured him. 'Although most practices do operate an emergency system for this sort of problem, as you're here, I might as well deal with it straight away.'

'What will you do?' Now that he'd been reassured that he wasn't going to be turned away, the patient's uncertainty about what was going to happen to him resurfaced.

'Initially, I'll inject with some painkiller but, because the abscess is so extensive, it probably won't be completely successful. The nerves under the muck inside will probably still be screaming at you, although the skin won't feel a thing.'

'Then what?' He was following the preparation going on around him with morbid fascination.

'Then I'll make an incision in your skin to drain the poison out, possibly putting a wick in to stop it healing over before we've got it all. Then it'll be dressed and we'll send you off with some antibiotics and an appointment to have the drain removed and a stitch put in to close the incision, if necessary.'

'Sounds simple enough,' he said then hissed when, in spite of her best efforts, the injection brought tears to his eyes.

The rest of the procedure was routine enough for Libby's brain to operate easily on two levels, one of them providing a step-by-step account of how things were proceeding, the other grieving over the fact that Nick had barely glanced in her direction over the last two days, let alone had a conversation with her, and it would take more than an injection of analgesic to deaden that sort of pain.

In the silent darkness of her bedroom she'd gone through every possible reason for his change of manner towards her.

The only thing she was certain of was that it had all stemmed from that conversation he'd had with Doug, and bearing in mind that he was a consultant oncologist, that brought a whole host of fears with it.

The worst was that he had told Nick that he was suffering from cancer and the thought that he might be dealing with that news alone, with his parents halfway around the world in Russia and no other close family for support, left her broken-hearted.

Surely he knew that she was here for him, no matter what the problem was? Surely he had some idea of her feelings towards him and that she would do anything for him?

Then it was time for the next patient and an excruciating half-hour working side by side with Nick while they tried to stabilise a patient who'd collapsed in the reception area before he'd even been able to give his name.

Even as they were examining him, his breathing worsened and he was losing control of his limbs, but for some reason it was the tingling sensation he reported in his face and tongue that rang a bell in Libby's mind.

'Is it Guillain-Barré syndrome?' she suggested as they fought to maintain his breathing.

'He's deteriorating too fast for us to waste time doing any definitive diagnosis down here,' Nick said shortly, somehow managing to remain aloof from her even though they were frantically working on the same patient. 'He needs to be on his way up to ICU straight away. He's going to need full life support any minute!'

It was almost a relief when Kelly took pity on her and sent her for a stint to help clear up a backlog at the minor injuries end of the department. The trouble was, dealing with an earring in a two-year-old's ear and a painfully strained wrist after a football accident wasn't enough to stop her from realising that her misery must be obvious to all if Kelly thought it a good idea to send her to the other end of the department.

The Colles' fracture that had resulted from a fall from a skateboard was straightforward, the break clearly identified from the characteristic dinner-fork deformity even before the X-ray was taken and the whole process of positioning the limb and applying a stabilising cast took long enough for Libby to come to an important decision.

As soon as her shift was over, she was going to find out where Nick had been hiding himself in his off-duty hours for the last couple of days. And once she had found him, she wasn't going to let him walk away until he'd answered some questions…such as why he had abandoned Tash when she'd come to rely on him to keep her daughter's spirits up.

Tash had been seriously downhearted when a second day had gone by without a visit from him, wondering whether she'd done something to upset him. Libby had made excuses for him, but inside she'd been furious and she wasn't go-ing to stand for it. If Nick had a problem, that was one thing, but he was an adult and if he was going to cut the youngster out of his life, then at least he was going to have to find the manners to tell her why.

As soon as she found him, Libby was going to insist on it.

'Nick!' Libby called after him as he strode towards the entrance, glad to be leaving the department at the end of such a stressful shift.

Just the sound of her voice was enough to send his spirits soaring, then he remembered why it had been so stressful working with her and they plummeted again.

The coward inside him urged him to run so that he could avoid her, anything to delay their next conversation because he still didn't feel ready for it.

The trouble was, eventually they were going to have to talk about his discovery, and the longer he delayed, the harder it was going to be to explain why he hadn't told Libby the news straight away. She was sure to put some negative motive to the postponement, perhaps thinking it meant that he didn't trust her.

Nothing could be further from the truth. It was just taking him longer than he'd expected to process the unexpected information and to decide what he wanted to do about it.

Well, his thinking time was over, if Libby had anything to do with it.

He continued walking until he was far enough away from the entrance not to attract attention then stopped, turning to face Libby as she hurried out of the building to catch up with him.

The determined expression on her perfect little face was so characteristic of the woman she'd become over the last few years that he actually found himself smiling.

How could he not have realised that there wasn't any hard decision to be made? He loved Libby and he loved Tash and if they would have him in their lives…

'I need to talk to you,' Libby announced as soon as she was close enough to speak without raising her voice. 'Have you got time now, or would you like to suggest another time?'

Suddenly he was impatient to find out his

fate. Delaying wasn't going to make any difference to the outcome.

'Now works well for me…but I thought you would be up with Tash.'

'It's partly because of Tash that I came looking for you,' she said grimly. 'She told me I had to ask you what she'd done to upset you so that you don't like her any more.'

Nick swore, glad that Libby couldn't understand Russian. 'I had no idea that she would put that interpretation on it.'

'At that age, most of their conclusions are egocentric,' she pointed out, then added wryly, 'I wouldn't be surprised if she thinks she's also responsible in some way for global warming, Third World poverty and the destruction of the rainforests.'

Nick chuckled at the absurdity of the idea, but somehow that bit of nonsense had broken the strained atmosphere between them and he found himself reaching for her arm.

'You're right,' he said with a sigh and a silent prayer that he would find the right words the next hour so that he didn't destroy his one chance at happiness. 'We do need to talk, but we may as well do it somewhere a bit more comfortable than the front steps of the hospital.'

At his suggestion, they picked up some fish and chips from the take-away around the corner and carried them, still tightly wrapped, to his house.

'What would you like to drink? I think the choice is tea, coffee, water or juice,' he offered as he reached for two plates. 'I don't think I've got anything alcoholic in the house because I've run out of beer, and as it never seems worth opening a bottle of wine for one, I rarely buy any.'

'Water would be fine, unless you're boiling the kettle for something yourself,' she said as she reached out a hand to take the plates from him. 'I'll put the food on the plates while you deal with the drinks.'

With the two of them working together, it didn't take long before they were sitting down at a small table positioned to take full advantage of the view out of the window, framing first a rather neglected garden then a beautiful vista of fields and trees almost to the horizon.

Somehow, the fact that the lawn should have been mown a week ago was more endearing than offputting, and was certainly more in keeping with the patchwork of fields beyond his boundary than an aggressive mixture of designer steel, concrete and decking would be. It certainly played its part in calming him down before the imminent conversation.

Just when he'd decided that he couldn't put it off any more, it was Libby who took the bull by the horns.

'You've been avoiding me...and Tash...ever since Doug spoke to you the other day and... and I need to know...' She drew in a shuddering breath before she continued. 'Nick, did he tell you that you need treatment for cancer? Is that why you've been shutting me out...shutting *us* out?'

Nick swore under his breath, suddenly realising the enormity of what he'd put Libby through by leaving her wondering what was going on.

He leapt out of his seat and hurried round to take her hands to pull her up into his arms.

'No, Libby, no. It's nothing like that. *Nothing* like that at all.' He tightened his grip for a moment, relishing how dainty and fragile she felt in his arms as he rocked her even as he acknowledged that she was probably the least fragile woman he was likely to meet.

He remembered how she'd finally confided in him, not just about the assault that had led to her coma and amnesia but also about the fragmented nightmares that haunted her still. When he thought of everything she'd already overcome in her life…things that had made her stronger where many another would have collapsed under the burden…

What he couldn't predict was how she would react when he told her…

His thoughts were interrupted when she lifted her head from its comfortable position just below his chin and fixed him with those unforgettable blue-green eyes.

'Then tell me, Nick,' she challenged, almost

as if she'd been reading his mind. 'Tell me what's going on.'

'Doug Andrews had just had the results of the latest batch of volunteers hoping to match as bone-marrow donors for Tash.'

'And he wanted you to break the news because there still wasn't anyone suitable? Oh, Nick, it isn't your fault and, anyway, there's still time to look. Tash hasn't finished this course of chemo yet. If it puts her into remission we could have even longer for the search. We might not even need a donor if everything—'

'No, Libby. You've got it wrong,' he interrupted when he could get his voice under control. How like her it was that she would try to help him feel better about the supposed failure to find a match when she would be feeling so much worse. 'That's not what he wanted to tell me. It was the opposite, in fact. It's a very good match but, in line with hospital policy, unless they're direct blood relatives, recipients and donors don't usually know each other's names.'

'They've found a match!' she exclaimed, excitement lifting her voice nearly an octave and a broad smile stretching almost from ear to ear as she broke away from him to whirl in a mad circle. 'That's fantastic! And it's someone in the hospital…? In our own department…? Oh, Nick, are you really not allowed to tell me? I'd love to say thank you to whoever it is for being tested…for being willing to be a donor for Tash.'

'Calm down, Libby! Come back here.'

He grabbed her again and wrapped her in his arms, afraid that, if she reacted badly, this might be the last time she let him hold her. Still, it was difficult not to share her grin of elation even as he was trying to choose the right words to tell her what she wanted to know.

'I thought about it and knew that you deserve to know, because if things had been different…' He paused, not wanting to go into that aspect before he'd given her the good news. 'It's *me*, Libby,' he announced huskily, hoping she would be as happy as he was. '*I'm* the match for Tash.'

* * *

For a moment, Libby couldn't take in what Nick had said, then she couldn't believe that he'd said it.

This time it wasn't delight that had her whirling out of his arms, only to turn back to glare furiously up at him.

'You mean you've known for two days and it's taken you this long to decide to tell me?' she accused, now torn between celebration of Tash's good fortune and a sudden desire to hit the man. 'What on earth took you so long? Surely you knew that I'd be over the moon that I didn't have to worry about—'

'Libby, that isn't the only thing I need to tell you,' he interrupted seriously, reaching out to her again, but she wasn't ready to forgive and forget yet. 'Can we sit down, please, because this next bit involves some explanation, and—'

'More secrets?' she challenged with a combative lift of her chin, but she did return to her seat at the table. How could she not when she wanted to hear what he had to say?

His knuckles were white as they gripped his

rapidly cooling mug of tea and he seemed to be concentrating on counting every one of the golden blond hairs on the back of his hand as he sorted his thoughts out, making Libby more worried than ever about what was coming.

This should have been such a wonderful moment, to know that they had the option of a bone-marrow graft for Tash. Now…

'How much do you remember of your time at med school?' he asked suddenly. 'I mean, how big are the holes in your memory?'

'As far as I know, I didn't lose any of my work information because I passed all my exams,' she said, wondering why he was raising that topic when she'd expected…well, she didn't really know what she'd expected.

'And what do you remember of your social life at that time?'

This time she wasn't so comfortable answering, knowing that it was only because she'd been invisible to him that he didn't remember what a loner she'd been.

'I didn't have a social life. I was too busy

studying,' she said shortly. 'Anyway, I wasn't really into boys and dating. They weren't interested in me and I wasn't interested in them.' Well, how could she have been when there had only been one person who'd made her heart beat faster?

'You might not remember it, but that was only true until just before we reached the halfway point on the course,' he announced, and rocked her back in her chair.

'There was someone who was interested in you...he'd been interested in you almost from the beginning but he'd been far too involved with his studies and trying to keep up with your grades to dare to take time off for a social life, much though he'd have liked to...'

'What? Who?' She tried to interrupt, but now that he'd started he was obviously determined to finish in his own way.

'Then, one night when the rain was absolutely hammering down, he saw some local tearaways steal your umbrella and leave you to get soaked, and he couldn't just leave you there like that.'

'That really happened?' Amazement flooded her as the images that had lived inside her head for so long came into clear focus. 'But I always thought that was a dream, not a memory…just wishful thinking.'

She blushed when she realised what she'd just admitted, then grew even hotter when she remembered the intimate details of some of her other dreams. They couldn't be memories, too…

Or could they?

CHAPTER TEN

LIBBY forced herself to meet Nick's eyes, wondering if she would be able to read the answer she needed there.

What she saw sent her pulse haywire but left her with even more questions than before.

'Tell me,' she pleaded. 'Tell me what happened, then maybe the nightmares will go away.'

'I don't know anything about the night you were assaulted,' he said quickly, and dropped his eyes down to the hands still strangling that same mug of cold tea. 'Libby, I've been feeling so guilty ever since you told me because we'd arranged to meet up to have a quick drink to celebrate making it to halfway, but I was delayed. When I got there, no one seemed to have seen you, so I thought maybe you'd gone back to your flat.'

He brought his eyes up to meet hers again. 'I looked everywhere. I was frantic because I couldn't find you,' he said, and she could see the echoes of the pain he'd suffered in his eyes. 'It was as if you'd vanished into thin air without a word to anybody, until I overheard one of the other students saying they'd heard that you'd transferred to another med school.'

'Oh, Kolya,' she breathed, so sorry that she'd put him through that, even though she hadn't known she'd been doing it at the time.

'That's what you used to call me,' he said with the start of a smile. 'I told you it was my mother's nickname for me—the Russian diminutive of Nikolai—and somehow it became your name for me too.'

'So…' Oh, she had so many questions that it was difficult to know where to start. 'How long were we…together? How well did we know each other before I…?'

'We had been going out for three weeks—if

that's what you can call it when we spent most of our free time together studying,' he added in a wry aside, then immediately grew sober again and reached out one hand as though he wanted to take hers. As though he lost his courage it came to rest on the table just inches from making contact.

'It didn't seem like three weeks, Libby. It felt...it felt as if we'd always known each other...as if we were meant to find each other.'

The intensity of his words and his expression sent a shiver up her spine, and every nerve ending seemed to be quivering with awareness so that she couldn't wait for him to continue.

'Did we...? Were we...?' She couldn't say it! How stupid was that? She was a doctor who saw naked bodies every day of the week and had to probe humanity's most intimate secrets and she couldn't...

'Yes,' he whispered, answering the question she couldn't put into words, and she saw his eyes darken with memories.

Were they the same memories that appeared

in her dreams, the ones that left her feeling bereft and breathless when she woke up in the
morning? Hers were so fragmented that sometimes they barely made sense. Could he remember everything? Every kiss, every touch, every
murmured endearment?

'We were sleeping together right from the beginning,' he told her, his voice growing husky
with emotion. 'It was so...so explosive...so
perfect...so inevitable...'

There was so much passion in his words, in
his eyes, that she felt almost seared by it, and it
was only by dragging her thoughts back to the
whole reason for their conversation that she
stopped herself from joining him on his side of
the table to see if they could re-create a few of
their most memorable scenes.

'So, why didn't you say anything when we
first started working together at St Luke's? It's
been weeks since we...'

'Obviously you still don't know enough about
the male ego,' he said with a wry chuckle. 'Let
me widen your education. Number one...' He

held up one lean finger, the nail scrupulously short and clean. 'We don't like being beaten by brainy women. Now, I know it's not your fault you were given more brains than most and I know it's not logical, but that still doesn't mean we don't have a problem with coming in a distant second. And number two...' A second finger joined the first. 'We don't like being dumped—*so* bad for the ego. Now, not having had extensive experience of the phenomenon, I wouldn't know whether it was worse to be dumped without ever knowing the reason why or to be dumped for another bloke or even dumped for another woman...'

By that time Libby was giggling, captivated by his nonsense even as she recognised the serious intent behind it.

'Message received and understood,' she said through her chuckles. 'In future, I'll try to act like a dim light bulb when in your company.'

'*Yelizaveta*, no one could ever mistake you for a dim light bulb, no matter how hard you tried. That's why...' He paused and sighed. 'That's why I tried to keep my distance for a couple of days, until I got my head around everything. Otherwise you'd have known that there was something I wasn't telling you.'

The word he'd used sounded far too musical to be one of his infamous curses, and she would have to ask him about it later. First, she needed to get all the secrets out in the open.

'You said that you needed time to decide whether to reveal that you were the match for Tash, but I don't think that's the whole truth,' she said quietly. 'There's definitely something else…'

'See. That's what I told you. Too bright by half,' he complained equally softly. 'And you're right about there being something else.'

'Something that Doug told you? Something that would stop Tash receiving your bone marrow?'

'No. The opposite, if anything.' He leant forward to catch both her hands in his, the mug of cold tea finally abandoned. 'Libby, he told me that the match was so good that if he didn't know differently, he would have thought that Tash and I were father and daughter.'

Libby felt her eyes widen as the implications sank in. Suddenly, the huge weight that she had been carrying around ever since she'd discovered that she was pregnant seemed to tumble from her shoulders.

'Tash isn't the result of a rape?' she breathed, torn between tears and laughter. 'She's *your* daughter? But...'

'We took precautions when we made love, knowing that having a baby at that stage of our training could be disastrous, but, well, they do say that nothing is foolproof. We could do a DNA test if you want to be certain,' he offered. 'But I certainly don't need one to know that she's mine.'

That was enough to start the tears flowing, and in an instant Nick had scooped her out of her chair and carried her through to the sitting room.

'Don't cry, *Yelizaveta*. We still have so much to talk about...plans to make...'

'What was that you called me?' she sniffed. 'You said it earlier, too.'

'Yeh-lee-zah-VYE-tah,' he pronounced slowly. 'That's Elizabeth, in Russian, and it was my *babushka*'s...my grandmother's name. And while Tash is a shortened form of Natasha, you might not know that it's the Russian nickname for someone with my mother's name, Nataliya.'

'You mean, I managed to name my daughter after your mother, even when I couldn't remember...'

'You see,' he teased, 'how difficult it could be for us mere mortals to compete with such effortlessly clever people.'

His banter helped her tears to dry and it was then that she noticed just how comfortably settled she was in his arms at one end of a luxuriously enormous settee.

She sat very still for a moment, soaking in the novel feeling of being cherished and cared for. Only in her dreams could she remember what this had felt like...strong arms cradling her against a broad chest with her head nestling perfectly in the angle between shoulder and neck as though it had been made just for her.

The difference in their heights, so noticeable

when they were standing, completely disappeared when they were together like this, and all she would have to do was turn her head and tilt her chin and she would be able to press her lips to his.

It was a delicious thought but before she could act on it they heard one of their pagers shrill out its summons.

'It's in the kitchen so it's mine,' Libby groaned as she reluctantly disentangled herself from Nick's hold and hurried off in search of her bag.

'I hope they don't think they're going to call you in this evening. You're a long way down the list if they're short of personnel.'

'It's not A and E, it's Oncology,' Libby gulped, terror flooding her heart in an instant. 'Something's happened to Tash. Something's gone wrong with the chemo.'

'Phone and find out before you kill yourself with a heart attack, trying to guess why they've contacted you,' Nick advised, handing her his phone, but Libby noticed that he was several shades paler than he'd been a couple of minutes ago, too.

'This is Libby Cornish answering a page from Oncology,' she announced when she got through to the number displayed on her pager.

'Just a minute. Mr Andrews wanted to have a word with you,' said the efficient voice on the other end.

'Did he want me to come in? Is there a problem with my daughter's treatment? She's Tash…Natasha Cornish. I could be there in a matter of minutes if he needs me to—'

'Libby, it's Doug Andrews here.' His steady voice interrupted her terrified gabbling. 'Now, stop panicking! I *didn't* contact you to give you bad news.'

His reassurance stopped her in her tracks and made her feel so weak that she had to use the nearest wall to stop herself collapsing on Nick's kitchen floor.

Suddenly those supporting arms were around her again, pulling her back against the lean strength of his body, caring and comforting and just…*there*.

'You didn't?' she squeaked, then had to clear

her throat. 'So if it isn't bad news about Tash, what is it?'

'How about some good news for a change?' he suggested, and without terror clouding her mind she could hear from his voice that he had a broad smile on his face. 'How about the fact that we just had a set of tests back and they're absolutely textbook perfect for this stage of the chemo?'

'No! Really? Textbook perfect? I can't believe it...not after all the disappointment with the first course. But what about the down side?' she asked warily.

'None showing up on any of the tests so far,' he reassured her.

'You're sure?' she demanded, too accustomed to things going wrong in her life to be able to accept success easily.

'Libby, the results are encouraging enough that I'm about to leave for home and take my wife out for a meal to celebrate,' he told her, and he sounded so positive that she finally allowed herself more than a glimmer of hope. 'Now, I suggest you do something similar and then get a good night's sleep. I have a feeling it's not going to be long before that little girl of yours is going to be firing on all cylinders and you'll need all your energy to keep up with her.'

'Did you hear that, Kolya?' she demanded as she put the phone down and twisted in his arms to face him, hardly aware that she'd used that long-ago nickname so easily. 'Did you hear what he said?'

'Every beautiful word!' he exclaimed. 'That's why I had my head pressed right against yours.'

'The chemo's finally working! Isn't it wonderful?'

'Fantastic!' he agreed, his smile every bit as wide as hers. 'And it's definitely something worth celebrating…on doctor's orders. Come here…' And he lifted her off her feet and whirled her in a circle before bending his head to give her a kiss.

At first their lips spoke of relief and delight that Tash's health was finally on the mend, but that quickly changed until Libby couldn't think at all.

She was disappointed when he ended the kiss.

It might have started as a celebration of Tash's good news but it had become something so much more that she would have been quite happy to have continued indefinitely, but suddenly he was untangling their bodies then startled her by stepping back from her, only to sink to one knee.

'Marry me, Libby,' he demanded, his breathing still unsteady after the passion of their kiss and she had a sudden picture inside her head of something very similar happening a long time ago. 'I know you've only got my word for it, but we first started planning our future together years ago, and even when I thought I'd lost you for ever, I knew I'd never be able to love anyone else the way I love you. We've got a lot of time to make up and I don't want to waste any more of it. Marry me, soon.'

Libby didn't know it was possible to be so ecstatic. Kolya's proposal made everything almost perfect.

'I'd love to marry you…on one condition,' she said with a joyful smile as she pulled him up from his knees and reached up to wrap her arms around his neck.

'Anything you want. Just name it,' he promised blithely.

'That you re-create our first time together so we can both share the memories.'

He chuckled richly, clearly delighted by the idea. 'I can't guarantee that I can call up a rainstorm on cue, nor do I want those yobs stealing your umbrella again, but as for the rest of that night…it will be my pleasure.'

'Don't worry, Libby. Tash will be fine with us,' Leah ffrench promised, son Ethan snuggled up fast asleep against the shoulder of her matron-of-honour dress.

'Yes. If she gets tired of playing with Ethan, she can always come over and entertain Megan,' Maggie offered, her teething daughter trying to chew a hole in her matching outfit.

'Yeah, Mum. I'll be fine,' Tash said, as she hopped eagerly from one foot to the other, her hair not much longer than the two babies', but at least it was growing back thick and healthy after the chemotherapy. 'You and Dad can go on your honeymoon. You need to get started on getting me a sister.'

'There are no prizes for guessing who put her up to saying that,' Libby said, resigned to the fact that everyone was going to be watching her waistline from now on...including Kolya. 'Nick's parents have been complaining that they missed out on all the baby cuddles the first time round.'

'They aren't the only ones campaigning either,' Leah groaned with a telling glance over her shoulder towards her in-laws, recently arrived from New Zealand to stay. 'At least David's parents have finally sorted out their problems. I doubt that his mother will ever be able to stop herself doting on her precious son, but at least with so many grandchildren to dilute the attention...and his father finally learning to put his foot down...'

She didn't need to say any more, especially not in front of Tash, but all three women had heard about the cataclysmic showdown when David had told his parents of Libby's existence.

The biggest surprise had been that, while the guilt he'd been feeling all those years for breaking his marriage vows had stopped him from putting his foot down sooner, David's father had finally been driven to point out to his wife that it had been her obsessive behaviour that had driven him into his secretary's arms. He'd declared that Libby, his long-lost daughter, was the totally innocent victim of the whole situation and had welcomed her into the ffrench family wholeheartedly, and he hadn't given his wife any option but to do the same.

Anyway, the first time Libby and her daughter had been introduced to the couple after their return from New Zealand, Tash had completely captivated the older woman in a matter of minutes with her mixture of innocence and vivacity, clearly delighted to have acquired an extra grandmother.

'Do you need any help changing out of your dress before you leave?' Leah offered. 'Have you got everything ready to go away?'

'Everything's ready and it won't take me more than five minutes to change.' She gestured towards her dress, a plain column of ivory silk. 'You might have noticed that I'm not really into over-elaborate dresses.'

'It might not have all the frills and flounces but you couldn't have chosen anything that suited you better,' Maggie said generously. 'The colour is perfect with your dark hair and the style and the way the fabric hangs make you look slender and elfin and... Oh, I'm never going to be able to loose the podge I put on when I was carrying Megan!'

'Wasn't she worth it?' Leah asked pointedly.

'Of course she was, every ounce of it,' Maggie conceded, and deposited a loving kiss on her daughter's downy head. 'Just you wait, Libby. It won't be long before you're—'

'Before she's in the car, being whisked off to a romantic honeymoon destination,' her brother interrupted, his timing perfect to spare Libby's blushes. 'Libby, I'd suggest that you disappear off and change or our parents are never going to let your husband escape and you'll miss out on your honeymoon.'

Your husband...

Libby felt a shiver of delight shimmy its way up her spine at those special words. Across the room, as though he knew she was thinking about him, Kolya lifted his head from his conversation with David's parents and met her eyes.

It was time to go, his expression told her. There were too many people around them for what they both wanted to do...for Kolya to fulfil the promise he had made on the day he'd asked Libby to marry him.

Despite the temptation to let their passion run its course, they had decided to wait for their wedding night before he re-created their first night together, and in just a few short hours...

'Whew! Can anyone else feel the heat between these two?' Maggie teased. 'Much more of this and they'll spontaneously combust!'

Libby laughed at her nonsense but her cheeks were burning as she hurried off to change.

* * *

'So, exactly how much *do* you remember about that first time?' Kolya asked as Libby tried to unlock the suitcases that had already been delivered to their room with trembling hands. 'Anything at all?'

She'd been surprised when a bout of last-minute shyness had struck her the moment she'd entered the sumptuous suite and seen the vast canopied bed, her brain hardly functioning beyond the significance of the two of them in this room together.

'Well, it certainly didn't happen in a room like this!' she joked uneasily.

'Ah, but you must admit, the weather outside is exactly right,' he pointed out, as the sound of rain hammering down outside the windows intensified. 'Do you want to go out on the balcony to get in the mood?'

'You mean, do I want to re-create the "drowned rat" look for authenticity? I don't think so,' she objected. 'Not in a pure silk dress! And, anyway, you haven't brought your umbrella with you to rescue me.'

'So, am I already a tarnished white knight…a failure on my first quest?' he asked despondently.

'Be not down-hearted. Your quest isn't over yet, Sir Knight,' she pointed out, grateful that his nonsense had dispelled her attack of nerves so easily. Now all she could feel was anticipation and desire. 'I'm sure you can manage to redeem your honour.'

'It won't be for lack of trying,' he murmured as he finally slid his arms around her and lifted her off her feet, turning to press her against the nearest wall. 'So, exactly how much do you remember of our first time together? Does this ring any bells?'

The picture inside her head was very clear from the number of times she'd dreamed the scenario. She remembered very clearly the way they'd laughed and stumbled their way into the small entrance hallway outside her one-roomed flat to get out of the rain; the way they'd both grown silent as he'd stared down into her eyes as though he'd never be able to look away again; the way her pulse had been beating so fast and so hard that she had been certain he had to be able to hear it, terrified that this might be all she would ever have of him. And then he'd groaned and swept her up into his arms and pressed her against the dingy wall for their first kiss…the kiss she'd been craving since the first time she'd seen him.

'It's not quite the same,' she pointed out, a quiver of anticipation in her voice. 'As I remember it, the first time you didn't bother wasting any breath talking…you got straight on with the kissing.'

'Your wish is my command, my lady,' he whispered as he angled his head towards hers.

'Are you ready to cry "Mercy!" yet?' Nick gasped as they both fought for breath among the tangled bedclothes several hours later.

'I didn't cry "Mercy!" last time, did I?' she pointed out as she ran admiring fingertips over his impressive six-pack then slid them down his taut belly to tangle in the thick tawny hair beyond. 'It was just the fact that we both had to get to the hospital that…'

Her words dwindled to a halt when she realised what she'd just said, and the increased tension in the long lean body beside her told her
that *he'd* picked up on what she'd just said, too.

'You remember that?' he asked softly, almost
as if he was afraid that speaking too loudly would
shatter any fragile connections being restored.

'I don't know,' she said honestly. A feeling of
utter peace spread through her and she knew
she had to try to explain.

'For as long as I can remember, there's always
been something missing from my life. When I
was little, it was the fact that I only had Mum,
then at school the fact that I was brighter than
average tended to set me apart. It was the same
at med school.'

'Apart from the fact that you only had eyes for
me,' he teased wickedly.

'Hmm! I've a nasty feeling that I should never
have told you that,' she muttered, throwing him a
dark look. 'But, unfortunately, it's true, and I still
measured every man against you even though I
couldn't remember the time we'd spent together.'

'Which brings us back to my original question,' he pointed out, trapping her wandering hand before it could take its exploration any further. 'About familiarity and memories.'

'And I don't really know the answer,' she admitted. 'I don't know whether everything seems so familiar because we've spoken about it, because I'm actually remembering the first time, because it's the fulfilment of my fantasies or...or whether it's just perfect.'

'Does it really matter which it is?' He rolled over towards her and this time it was his turn to start the journey of discovery with gentle fingertips.

'No. It doesn't matter...' she said firmly when she realised that was nothing but the truth. 'The lonely place inside me—the part that longed for a family and friends—has disappeared because I'm totally surrounded by family now. Apart from the three of us—you, me and Tash—there are your parents, who are absolutely thrilled to be grandparents and are *already* hinting that the more grandchildren the merrier, then there's the ever-increasing ffrench family…'

'But?' he prompted when she paused, and she smiled at the way he'd been able to pick up on her underlying feelings.

'But even though I'm now surrounded by the family I've always longed for, the only thing that really matters is us and the love we've found.'

'*And* all the children we're going to create to share that love with?' he suggested with a wicked knowing grin when her breathing hitched in her throat at his intimate caresses. 'My parents are hoping to hear good news in the not-too-distant future.'

'Well, we wouldn't like to disappoint your parents,' she agreed, her concentration on their conversation slipping as he continued to arouse her. 'But it can take time to…to build the perfect family. It could take hours and hours of…of practice before we get it just right…'

'I suppose that's another of a knight's important duties?' His pupils were widely dilated now, evidence that he was every bit as aroused as she was.

'It could be a perilous undertaking and take many years, Sir Knight,' she warned on a gasp of pleasure.

'In which case, my lady,' he said in a husky voice as he leant forward to tease her lips with increasingly passionate kisses, 'we'd better not lose any time…'